Murielle's Angel

MARY HOWELL

CinnamonPress

INDEPENDENT INNOVATIVE INTERNATIONAL

Published by Cinnamon Press, Meirion House, Tanygrisiau, Blaenau Ffestiniog, Gwynedd LL41 3SU
www.cinnamonpress.com

ISBN 978-1-907090-83-7
British Library Cataloguing in Publication Data. A CIP record for this book can be obtained from the British Library.
Designed and typeset in Garamond by Cinnamon Press. Cover design by Jan Fortune from detail of original artwork 'camino de santiago countryside' by Loois McCartney © Loois McCartney, agency dreamtime.

Cinnamon Press is represented by Inpress and by the Welsh Books Council in Wales.
Printed in Poland
The publisher acknowledges the support of the Welsh Books Council

Murielle's Angel is a work of fiction, Any resemblance to any person is entirely co-incidental.

I am indebted to Stephen Foster, to Gwen Davies of the Welsh Arts Council for her assistance to Jan Fortune and to my long suffering family, without whose help none of this would be possible.

For Denis

ONE

A couple joined the train as it rattled through Spain for the French border. Rosemary stared anxiously. Had they no inkling how they looked? At home some youth would have sniggered at them striking out in their plus fours and capes and pixie hats, with their wooden staves clanking with scallop shells. Some old woman would have challenged then on their clumsy way through the carriage as their rucksacks knocked into every passenger. No one else gave them a second glance. Had they no inkling of how they looked? Perhaps their clothes had been handed down through generations of pilgrims or, more worryingly, perhaps all pilgrims dressed this way and this epic walk would be peopled with outlandish types and she would be out of place in her dress and sensible sandals. She pictured them with their family dressed in their ridiculous clothes; the family would nod, smile knowingly. 'Off on pilgrimage?'

How difficult it had been to explain her need for escape. A dress code would have announced 'Pilgrim Mode' and the phrase, 'The time has come, see you in a couple of months, maybe,' would have rolled off the tongue.

The train slowed on the outskirts of Pamplona and when the odd couple made a move to get off she did too, thinking to learn from them how to be a pilgrim. In the confusion of the busy station they evaporated like will o' the wisps. She felt, for a moment, as an explorer might on the eve of some great mission: not excitement, but a sense of doom. The preparation for the walk, having required a show of confidence that would blind onlookers to the obvious flaws in an otherwise great plan, had mostly been bravado. There had been no research, no testing of equipment; no practice walks with a laden rucksack; in fact, no practice walks at all. The rucksack had sat like an unwelcome guest in the spare bedroom, its zips and clasps unavoidably loud and accusing in the chill of the unused room as she had furtively packed and repacked.

Once hoisted, the rucksack governed every movement, its presence an unwieldy carapace like Kafka's dung beetle. The embarrassment of it worried away with the burden of its weight and the chafing of her shoulders in an effort to put one foot in front of the other. She was tempted to shed half the contents as she passed a post office in the busy town; wrap them and send them forward; even bin them: anything to lighten the load. She thought of the Chinese proverb about the longest journey that starts with the smallest step and trudged to find Tourist Information to obtain the necessary documents. That much she knew: a pilgrim needed documents.

Inside, a smiling school-age girl asked her why she wanted to walk the Camino de Santiago. 'None of your damn business,' would have been her gut reply had she not seen the long list of answers from previous pilgrims: it was a question that had been posed to them all. The girl gave a choice: spiritual or sport; and down the length of the page the girl, or a colleague, had written either spiritual or sport beside each name, *espiritual, deportivo.*

The question unlocked a mental filing cabinet of reasons. *I am walking because I can't go on this way or that way or any way at all. I am just walking, OK?* The question might equally have been 'Why are you breathing?' as relevant and as difficult to answer. The girl smiled expectantly with her pen poised over the register, a vast tome like a book of judgment with page after page of names and nationalities with *espiritual* or *deportivo* hand written beside them.

Why would anyone wish to know this detail? Where did completed registers go and who counted the results? Perhaps it was a job given to prisoners or the long term unemployed or school leavers. 'Here is your introduction to the world of work: mind numbing, pettifogging and utterly pointless.' There would be dark, underground rooms with row after row of heads bowed in submission and enormous disappointment, counting and entering numbers in columns. And there it was: the reason for the limit of two choices. It was simply for ease of gathering statistics that choices were reduced to either/or. Life without *what ifs* should be a skill to practise, an exam to pass before being released into the world.

She watched the care with which the girl entered her details: Rosemary Wallace; age: 48; and *espiritual* filled the entry in the logbook. Then the young girl asked her nationality and was surprised by the answer.

'Engleesh?' the girl said with a smile, 'the only one.'

Rosemary had not assumed the walk would teem with compatriots, but she had expected to meet one or two. When she had mentioned nonchalantly to select girl friends that she was thinking of walking a pilgrimage in Spain, alone, she had met with a mix of envy, admiration for her bravery and total ignorance.

She smiled back feeling patriotic: a bone fide Engleesh pilgrim.

She needed a *credencial* from the bishop's Palace.

'It is your *pasaporte* to the *hostales*. No *credencial*, no can stay.'

Directions to the *palacio arcobispal* were given in

7

Engleesh and were a little difficult to follow.

Cobbled streets grew narrower and shade deepened as medieval buildings leaned in with the passing of years so that only a thin strip of blue remained overhead. The air grew almost chill. Ageless people with mangy dogs and dirty fingernails loomed in doorways, their hair felted by rough, dream filled nights. One final turn led to a dark alley. A young man fell into step behind her and she sensed his eyes on her rucksack. She was not about to be mugged for her oldest pairs of knickers and a few sorry tee shirts. She turned to confront him, thinking that he would be less brave face to face. He walked meekly past with his head down as if he had not even seen her and there behind him was a sign for the Archbishop's Palace.

The entrance arch to the palace was so dark that it took some moments for her eyes to adjust. A face looked down on her from a tiny opening, an illuminated talking gargoyle, telling her to come on up. The face withdrew leaving no trace of the window and no apparent way of entering. She groped her way along the wall and eventually found the entrance. Her carapace caught on the narrow staircase as she heaved herself up.

The official, a mild mannered, apologetic man, was almost completely encased in plaster, his arms stuck at the angle of a farm labourer with a staff across his shoulders. He must have been craned in to the office. Rosemary had to leave the rucksack outside the entrance as there was not enough room for the three of them. It seemed all he could do comfortably was talk, so he directed while she found and stamped the necessary passport.

He had fallen downstairs after a party and broken

8

many bones. She raised her eyebrows in commiseration and to indicate that she knew how it could be after a good party.

'You are very lucky,' he told her, 'You have the special bishop's stamp for your *credencial*, it is highly prized. Tomorrow I will close the office.'

'Are you in a lot of pain?' she asked.

'No, I am getting married tomorrow.' And he gave a look that suggested he would have shrugged his shoulders had they not been immobilised.

She wished him good luck and left him encased in peace. He wished her *Buen Camino*: Good Way: the way of St James. She liked the play on the word that made it less of a highway, more a way of life that she had chosen for the next few weeks.

She walked away from streets, cars, shops, bustle, into the quiet of a deserted, dusty road, no more than a track, yellowing into the distance. There was no sign that it was the right track, although her shadow reassuringly kept pace: just the two of them on the road. The only sounds were the plock of her stick and the friction of her bag as they struggled to find a comfortable way of being together. Now up hill, now down, the undulations did nothing to mitigate the pain of feet and shoulders. She thought of crying at the folly of it, *What ever it is you're trying to prove, you've made your point,* but no tears came.

As she reached the brow of the hill a gentle rustle of wind caused her to look up. A pilgrim, dressed from head to foot in black, was momentarily silhouetted against the evening sky. He stood with a stave in one hand and the hump of a knap sack on his back. The sun glowed behind him, a vision of great import but then he was gone. The impression was so brief and had such a timeless feel that she

9

could not be entirely sure it had been real. When she had chosen *espiritual* as her reason for making a pilgrimage, she had not envisaged a *mystic* experience merely one that would be reflective. Had she chosen *deportivo* perhaps her first image would have been cyclists in neon coloured leggings and helmets. It was as if the mere choice of words had set her on an entirely different path.

The relentless sun, considerably lower in the sky, had gone behind a church tower. *Espadañas* they are called in Spanish, those square towers with a gap for the bell that tolls in cowboy films when the village is in danger. A huge, untidy stork's nest perched beside the bell. A yellow arrow painted on the road pointed towards a hostel, a large stone house and several outbuildings in a field, set back along a gravel drive. There were some fruit trees providing shade and a view looking over a vast plain. People were sitting here and about and the breeze wafted with murmuring and the scratch of pens on paper.

She was absurdly grateful that she could legitimately stop walking and put down her rucksack, easing it from her shoulders and letting it drop with a crunch. She scrabbled for the *credencial* from the top pocket and stood with it in her hand. She waited with two or three other pilgrims by a table set up outside the open French windows of the house. No one spoke. Presumably, la Señora would come and stamp their passports and tell them what to do. After a few moments, when no one came and still no one spoke, Rosemary looked about and decided the whole place was sleepy; siesta not yet over. La Señora lay reading on a chaise-longue within easy reach of the table and when she looked up as she turned a page, she momentarily fixed her gaze on the queue before returning to read as if that stare should be message enough. The two or three shuffled away and Rosemary moved her bag in to partial shade and lolled on it, suddenly worn out after barely three hours' walk.

Time stretched. She had thought of sight seeing in Pamplona; looking for a plaque, 'Hemingway slept here,' or 'Bull Running this way,' but had abandoned any thought the instant the rucksack had been hoisted and the weight of it had begun to dig into her shoulders. Now she regretted it. She wrote in her notebook, 'Day One,' underlined it and drew a daisy, then put it back in her bag. She looked for the book she had brought with her to read, with its optimistic, jaunty title, *As I walked out One Midsummer Morning* and realised she must have left it on the train. She took out her guidebook and tried in vain to plan an itinerary. The route, drawn by a thick red line slicing through Northern Spain had the names of towns and villages along the way written at right angles to it like teeth in a zip. She ran her fingers up and down it on the page half expecting to feel crenellations, but found it impossible to concentrate and resorted simply to staring at the view: a vast landscape dancing in the heat. Somewhere ahead lay the path for the next day and she thought she might at least look for that, but the languor of siesta was infectious and she stayed semi-recumbent and her lids grew heavy.

TWO

A pilgrim approached. He was tall, greying at the temples with pale, intelligent eyes and affable good looks like a film star. *Soy José Luis*, he bowed slightly making a gesture to ask if she would mind if he sat with her. She didn't mind.

'I'm Rosemary,' and she smiled.

He repeated her name, but did not attempt to pronounce it the English way.

Rosa Maria, encantado.

Encantada: the word felt good in her mouth.

He asked to see her guidebook. *Inglesa?* Sadly, he did not understand English, but he had heard of this English guidebook. He weighed it in his hand indicating that he approved of its lightness. He showed his photocopied pages from the Spanish guide and explained that after each day he used the blank reverse to write home to his son. He liked to write poetry, he said.

'I have a son,' she hesitated, 'he is twenty three, just finished a degree.' She thought of her son's reaction if she were to write poems home to him; more proof she'd gone bananas, perhaps. But the fact was she could not imagine his reaction because she could not imagine being close enough to him to write poetry in the first place.

There was no sign in José Luis' handsome face of any intention other than telling his tale. His manners were of a bygone age. She imagined him tilting at windmills and rescuing damsels. He was a widower, but not lonely; a retired pilot. He spoke of his joy of walking the Camino that he had walked many times before.

'It is a beautiful thing, *El Camino*.'

This time, he said, he was praying for strength and for a job for his son who was also a pilot, but was out of work. His soft voice filled the air and although she listened she was also with her own family whom, it now seemed to her, she had abandoned with unseemly haste. His words created a widening gap within her, as if, like a surgeon about to operate, he was opening her up with a surgical wrench and exposing in the beam of his head torch some rot that needed to be removed.

It began to grow chilly and La Señora was up and at her desk with a growing queue of pilgrims, ten or fifteen people had already lined up with more coming behind, some newly arrived from the brow of the hill. Arms were folded, rucksacks lent against brown, well-muscled legs and boots crunched gravel as the queue inched forward. José Luis suggested they join the queue, insisting with a little bow that she went before him.

Hushed tones gave way to raised Dutch and German voices, an argument brewing, a diplomatic incident between nations. The queue went quiet with the strain of listening for tell tale signs of escalation. José Luis raised his eyebrows as if to say this was totally uncalled for, then followed her to the front with a judicious use of elbows as the queue broke down, all jostling for a better view. A posse formed round the argument.

A belligerent finger was jabbing a bony shoulder with an unpleasant accusation that sounded like *puntlig unt gruntlig*. The belligerent finger belonged to a young man whose flop of blond hair bounced with every prod. The young man was so much shorter than his opponent that any moment the tall guy might cuff him like a lion chastising an annoying cub.

'Oh that insult is not too serious,' a voice from behind translated.

She turned to see a man smiling down from a great height. His arms folded over his chest were knotted with muscles like a Genie's from a lamp. He was dressed head to foot in black and immensely tall. She gazed up and up. The sun framed his head so she could not see his face, just a turban of blond hair.

'What's up with them?' she asked.

'They are arguing about guide books and which nationality has the best version.'

José Luis looked to her to translate. He threw his hands up in momentary disgust that anyone should argue so vehemently over nothing. Then, like a man who has full confidence in his orthodontist, he threw his head back and laughed, exposing strong white teeth.

Qué ridículo! Laughter escaped from the phrase.

The translator with the turban hair pointed to the green guidebook that Rosemary had tucked into her waistband and said,

'Show them yours, that'll shut them up.'

She could almost imagine how it would be. She would stiffen her upper lip, step forward and march to the front where la Señora, the camp commandant, would have put down her pen on the verge of unbuttoning her revolver to settle the matter; at the very least about to refuse privileges. Silence would fall. People would stand back to allow her to pass, closing the gap in her wake. She would tap the small jabber on the shoulder and he would stop abruptly mid prod and eye her. She would proffer her guidebook, like the diminutive British hero, Johnny Mills, saving the day, 'The best is British.' A murmur would pass through the small crowd; birds would

14

sing again, there would be laughter.

The jabber backed down without any outside influence, perhaps realising size was against him. His face, that of a child, once red and distorted with anger, broke into a wide grin. La Señora continued to register pilgrims and the queue dwindled. Pilgrims disappeared in clusters into the succession of huts and outbuildings, laughing, with no sign of the tension there had been.

Every available space of the hut to which she was assigned was covered with bunks and makeshift beds. Less than a foot away in all directions, foreign men were going about their ablutions. Some had hung their socks at window bars to air; some had balanced bars of soap on the edge of soap dishes and lined them up on the window ledge as if warding off evil spirits. All had wrenched forward the tongues of their boots and were putting them neatly outside. She sat on her camp bed and wondered what to do. She felt as if she did not yet know the rules and any moment she would be denounced as an impostor.

José Luis rapped on the window near her bed and gesticulated for her to come outside. He was going to eat in the village where a bar catered for pilgrims.

'It will be a good meal and not expensive. You'll need energy to walk tomorrow.'

She allowed herself to be shepherded by him, glad of the diversion and the company. They entered a huge room in the village, like an old-fashioned schoolroom, set out with long trestle tables. Carafes of red wine and water, baskets of bread and bowls of salad sat at intervals along them. The room was stuffy. Sunlight poked through high windows showering glittering particles of dust on just and unjust alike. The noise of several languages spoken at

15

once reached the rafters like a Tower of Babel. Pilgrims were filing in to join those already seated. Bread was broken; tumblers of wine were poured. Great lines of pilgrims sat in anticipation of the meal to be served. When it came, all along the bench, heads bowed towards plates and food disappeared. Rosemary thought the meal was disappointing; cold, meagre and expensive.

José Luis and Rosemary sat near the belligerent pilgrim who was talking earnestly to the translator with the turban hair, who smiled at them in recognition revealing two lines of dimples and turned back to his conversation.

'Are you a pilgrim?' she asked him and immediately regretted it: a pointless question. He did not appear to have heard her or did not deign to answer if he had or even turn again to look. The conversation with José Luis, although equally one sided with him doing all the talking, was at least companionable.

She got into her sleeping bag fully-clothed without even cleaning her teeth and lay listening to the noises of the night: the restlessness of a thousand mice or were they rats? Scrabbling through plastic bags, sniffing through belongings, peeping through window bars. She lay, not waking, not sleeping in a hinterland between dreams and reality, living and reliving the past weeks, the past hours in a jumble of memories.

It was a lot to take in, an angry young man, a tall blond stranger, an avuncular Spanish poet. The walk she had known about since her youth; a dream, an ambition filed away that she had assumed, with all the presumption of youth, was something to attempt one day. The hope of achieving it faded with youth

16

and exuberance had rekindled on finding a leaflet among keepsakes and had burned incandescent. No scorn could quench it: *You think you can do what the hell you want, whenever the fancy takes you. Well the real world is not like that. You just bugger off and I'll pay for it.*

When she heard a cry in the night her mind was alert and briefly rational till sleep was inevitable and the cry merely a signpost in a dream. The subconscious aware of tales of the unquiet, of banshees luring sailors to their doom, keeps the heart beating fast, ready for flight. As the night settled back to no more than heavy breathing, sighs and rustles of a room of sleeping strangers and an animal starting way off, her heart steadied, disquieted but nothing. When she woke again the cry, a much more gentle sound, was definitely human. Somewhere in the large dormitory others were awake and had begun to talk quite low, a man and a woman. She could not make out what was being said, the words were foreign and conveyed nothing but the tone was urgent. She thought of messages gone astray, love affairs blighted with irreparable damage, or world shattering wars averted or prolonged.

'Send three and four pence we're going to a dance.'

Perhaps it was another argument or a thief caught going through the contents of someone else's bag. With the rhythmic creak and the beat of a head board against a wall came the understanding that the shout had been passion after all. Before she could begin to think of it, with the intake of the next breath, she had been asleep and dreaming again, unsure which was dream and which wakefulness. And in the morning with purposeful strangers zipping and unzipping bags and clothes she gave no thought to having been awake and forgot what it was

17

that she had almost heard.

She was surprised to find that the place was near deserted. It was barely half five and the silver morning already had the first wisps of dawn. Worried that she would lose her way in the half-light with no one to follow she rushed out without breakfast or even a wash and was enormously assured to see the strange humpback shadows of other pilgrims ahead of her and to hear the unmistakable plock of sticks on metalled road. The shadows disappeared silently, one by one, off the village street, slipping between granite houses to follow the yellow arrow and a narrow path over fields. The sun rose; a huge red ball over the endless plain, like the flag of Japan. The shadows that had been in front of her soon vanished in to the vast landscape and the whole world was hers; a world marked with yellow arrows, which, in the absence of people, were like talismans and were comforting to see.

THREE

After an initial descent the path broadened, winding its way along a wooded, undulating valley. Some pilgrims sat in the ruins of a church, already reaching for a drink and unwrapping packages of food. The place was dark and overhung with trees. The pilgrims looked as disconsolate as refugees and furtive, as if expecting marauders to steal their food. She hoped she might see José Luis' friendly face, someone with whom to greet the day, whose breakfast she could eye hungrily and accept graciously; but there was no one she recognised. She hunched her back and kept up a fast pace, hoping to establish a rhythm that might eliminate the discomfort in her shoulders.

She thought of the walk that lay ahead that day: 24 kilometres sounded a long way with sore feet getting sorer. She converted the distance to miles, dividing by eight and multiplying by five as her mother had taught her as a child when they had travelled abroad. Fifteen miles still seemed a long way. She calculated how many hours it would take at two and a half miles per hour. At least if the day started at five in the morning a six hour walk would be over before lunch. She tried to estimate how long the whole five hundred miles would take and then made mental calculations of her finances, which she had also learned to do as a child. The only conclusion she came to was that she should walk as fast and far as she could every day and spend as little as possible.

She was aware of someone behind her, but could not manage to shake them off. However much she quickened her pace, the follower would be behind; however much she slowed down the follower would

19

neither catch up nor overtake. Eventually she decided it was a deliberate ploy and, feeling almost threatened, turned to see who it was. The translator from the night before broke into a dimple-lined smile.

'I decided to walk with you today,' he said.

She kept a 'hmph' at his presumption to herself.

He introduced himself in good English and said that his name was Dominic, which was very unusual in Holland. She did not say anything.

'Dominique, nique, nique.' He sang the song that the Singing Nun had sung on *Top of the Pops* all that time ago. 'That is me.'

She laughed and remembering the song erased the pain where the rucksack had moulded to her shoulders; she was glad to leave off making any more calculations.

'We must be about the same age,' she said.

'I'm thirty seven.'

'Come off it. I'm forty eight and I look young for my age.'

He laughed. 'That's what I meant, *forty* seven.'

He chatted away, working hard at finding out about her. His hair bobbed up and down in the sunshine and beads of sweat fell from his face. He wasn't breathless and she wondered briefly if the sweat came from the effort of walking or the exertion of talking. Soon she had forgotten and simply enjoyed the warmth of the early morning and the company. She commented on how good his English was and he said it was easy for him; he was a Dutchman from a nation of linguists.

'We listen to everybody's radio and watch all their TV.' Almost as an afterthought he added, 'Your Spanish is good too,' and he smiled in acknowledgment of this compliment.

They spoke of childhood and things you learn without trying. He said he was one of eleven and came somewhere in the middle of his large family which sounded to her an easy place to lose oneself. His family had been poor and they only ever had boiled eggs for a treat when it was their birthday, and even then only the person whose birthday it was had the egg. She imagined cooking a dozen eggs at a time and spooning them into a row of eggcups one after the other.

'Are you a Catholic, Dominic?' she asked, surprised at the size of his family.

'I don't believe in God.' The reply was emphatic and his look implied that he found religion something reprehensible; something to grow out of.

'Are you?'

Catholicism was deeply engrained, so much of her early memories were tied up with it; church, school, and even home. Uncertain if she believed in anything anymore, it would be hard to stop being a Catholic.

'Probably.'

He seemed to find that answer amusing and his laugh was infectious.

Dominic was impressed by their speed, by hers in particular.

'It's easy for me, I have long legs.'

She studied them. They were surprisingly lean too, as if he had outgrown his strength as a youth. When they came to steep hills he altered his rhythm, as if changing gear. He had tried taking her hand and pulling her but it was no use. She simply could not keep up and she had been too out of breath. So he had slowed down but he had kept hold of her hand. When the path tipped down hill it felt as if they were flying.

21

He was a runner and spoke of running for hours through lovely Dutch countryside. Running had never appealed to her: pavement after pavement of foot bashing. Her street was one of strings of others that knotted the industrial north.

'Do you know Holland?'

'Windmills, clogs and tulips and the little boy with his finger in the dyke.'

Dominic did not know that story and she felt him grow tetchy as she teased him so she relented.

'A lovely few days in Amsterdam one spring and a walk through the red light district. That is all I know.'

He spoke of ice-skating when the canals froze in winter.

'We have a race, the eleven town's race. Every year we hope and we place bets. Will it be cold this year? Will a hundred and twenty five miles of canals freeze over? The farmers bring out their tractors to shine head lamps to light up the silver canal.'

'Have you skated the canals?' It sounded brave, daring, exciting.

'I went with my brother the last time it was cold enough. I was not so strong and had to stop, but he finished. Some houses near by make hot chocolate to give to the ones that don't make it. It is so cold even your hair freezes.'

'Why were you not so strong?'

'I was sickly as a boy. You do not think it to look at me now, huh? My mother never let me go out in the cold. The last big freeze maybe ten years ago, I thought, why not? This might be my only chance.'

She smiled and tried to picture him as a little boy kept indoors because of the cold.

'So are you walking this Camino for reasons of sport?'

'What *do* you mean?'

22

He made the inflection on the 'do' as if she was talking utter rubbish. She explained how she had been asked in Pamplona and given a choice of two possible answers. Dominic had not been asked this question. His walk had started in Roncesvalles with a blessing from a priest and the gift of a scallop shell, a coquille Saint Jacques. He had crossed the Pyrenees, which had been so difficult some pilgrims had turned back.

She examined the prospect of turning back. Giving up was not an option. They were quiet for some time, then Dominic said, 'Walking the Camino is very important to me.'

He felt it was almost a lifestyle choice; it was a turning point, a major event and he spoke at some length of all his preparations. Much research and planning had gone into his trip, which included a three-month sabbatical and a reconnaissance with his family. He had brought them for a holiday to Northern Spain so that they could imagine him walking and not miss him too much while he was away. He had driven them past the ancient paths that sometimes bordered main roads. She pictured stragglers from the army of pilgrims plodding in rags in retreat from their daily lives raising their heads to watch as blond haired children waved from the windows of a car being driven slowly past.

He had even organised events for his return, knew the date and had booked his flight. He had asked his wife to prepare a party when all the family would get together, all eleven of his brothers and sisters with wives, husbands, children and his mother. Everyone was proud of him. He would carry home the special Tarta de Santiago, a cake made of almonds, for them to share, as proof of his success.

'I want to celebrate it in style.'

How different from her departure. Dominic had exited in a blaze. She had felt the need for stealth, as if it was a shabby, unworthy thing, not a celebration. It was like a rebuke, although she knew it wasn't. How could Dominic know she had thrown things into a bag and fled the house deciding within a week to drop everything for a month or two? He had involved his family in his project. Perhaps this was how families should behave and such openness would create a desired closeness, a loving bond. She had involved no one; deliberately keeping quiet in case anyone should find good reason for her to postpone or cancel the trip.

There had been presents the morning of her departure. At breakfast her daughter, home especially for the weekend, handed her a beautifully wrapped travel set of peppermint foot lotion.

'You are coming back, Mum, aren't you?' Her grey green eyes were troubled.

'It feels as if we'll never see you again.'

Rosemary had been evasive. Her husband, Seb, had slid a small soft parcel across the table, too.

'This might come in.'

A travel towel: light, useful and so thoughtful. She'd had nothing to give to ease the parting, not even words.

'You don't want to miss your flight.'

Seb had put her heavy rucksack in the boot of the car. He hadn't smiled since she had told him of her plans and she had assumed that he was angry. The silence that had pervaded the house and the journey to the airport she also attributed to his anger. Seb did not want her to go; her place was at home; a Gina Lollabrigida to his Frank Sinatra; *barefoot and pregnant and in the kitchen.* And she knew she was being unfair. Hearing Dominic's account she admitted the anger

24

was hers. She could have made a joke; Seb would have appreciated the gesture. *For God's sake say something, even if it's just goodbye,* Humphrey Bogart or someone. But she had said nothing.

'Passivity is also aggression,' her brother in law had told her once, sensing her quiet resentment over some slight. Although she had not known this, she realised he was right.

'Tell that to your brother.'

'Isn't that the point, you should tell him,' he had looked hard into her eyes.

'We don't communicate.'

'I know you don't.'

FOUR

There were a couple of pilgrims on the path ahead walking slowly, a man and a boy, together but apart. They could hear talking, but it was not a conversation.

'He's using a dictaphone,' Dominic said.

As they drew near, alongside and then overtook, the man on the dictaphone kept up his monologue. His eyes fixed on some distant horizon; he was oblivious they were there. His companion was not a boy, but a woman who turned her head to stare blankly at Dominic and Rosemary.

'That poor woman,' Rosemary said when they were out of earshot.

'I know that self-obsessive type,' Dominic said. 'He'll be writing a book and later he'll play the tape back to himself just to hear his own voice. She will have the pleasure of listening all over again.'

'A dictaphone's not such a bad idea though, especially going along.'

'Are you writing a book about the Camino?' Dominic was suddenly animated.

'No, no I meant for him. Why, are you?'

Dominic was writing an article for a publication back home as people in Holland were interested in history, especially when it involved myth and legend. He too was fascinated by it.

'Have you read Edwin Mullins?' he asked.

'Never heard of him.'

'You must have heard of him; an English historian.'

The name sounded improbable to her. No one called Mullins could write and have his work taken seriously, surely? And she felt the old snobbishness of her mother and her aunt laughing behind their hands at someone's social gaffe at a polite tea party.

'No, never.'

'A definitive work about the Camino.'

'Besides, I don't do reading.'

And Dominic stopped and looked at her,

'Dyslexic?'

'No, of course not.' She relented, 'Emotionally dyslexic perhaps.'

'What is that? I don't know that term.'

'I just made it up, a self diagnosis, blind spots when it comes to other people.'

'I want to know about the reading.'

She was surprised that he should want to hear of her reading habits, thinking the new term she had coined much more interesting.

'My sister taught me to read and she hated me. It sort of rubbed off on the reading. I resent sitting still and I can't get lost in a book.'

Reading was something she did furtively, at night in those snatched moments before lights out. She thought of the delight of reading aloud to her children and the real reason why she did not read anymore rose in her mouth like bile. She rolled it round tasting it for effect, unsure whether to spit it out but unwilling to swallow it again.

'If you must know,' and the shame of saying it made her blush, 'my husband does not like me to read.'

Instead of recoiling at her weakness, Dominic leant towards her and kissed her cheek. She felt like a chosen one. The charismatic Dutchman, an undoubted leader of men who would have a following, wanted to talk to her and to listen, and yet she had nothing to say, was not well versed. The brush of his lips left a sensation on her cheek that

27

she wanted to touch, but did not want to appear to be wiping off. She tried to raise her shoulder to the spot, but the heavy bag prevented her. She decided that she was a bit in love with him.

'Tell me about Mullins, this chap you've made up.'

At first she enjoyed listening to tales of the Codex Calixtinus, a cross between medieval song book and travel log and the myths and miracles that surrounded the finding of the tomb of the apostle Saint James and the pilgrim route. The stories began to sound improbable: Charlemagne's vision describing where the body was to be found at the end of the earth, by following the Milky Way, the heavenly field of stars, *campus stellae,* which perhaps gave the town its name, and the headless St James riding into battle to rescue Spain from the Moors.

She had ceased to listen: the book by Edwin Mullins could be looked for on her return to England, but Dominic insisted.

Did she know that the myth of St James was a convenient political plot?

'No.'

Or that the term 'discovery/invention' was the delightful expression adopted by some historians and most ecclesiastics to explain the unorthodox, though timely, discovery of the Saint's remains and conveys the dilemma, *Is it true/ does it matter?*

Rosemary shrugged. 'Well does it matter if it's true?'

Dominic seemed exasperated. 'Of course it matters. Tens of thousands of people suspend their disbelief to participate in the cult of St James and walk at least part of the 500 miles to Santiago to say a prayer at his tomb.'

Did any of it matter? She was simply running away, she wasn't doing anything constructive:

emptiness and solitude was all she had in mind. She had given scant regard to St James the Apostle when she had decided to set off, although she had kept a picture of a twelfth century statue of St James, since school days. Perhaps the miracle was that the picture had resurfaced when she was seeking a way out.

When they stopped to rest, Rosemary felt the cold of drying sweat as she gingerly removed her rucksack. She had not once thought of blisters or aching back since she started to walk with Dominic. They sat in the dust of the empty path and her eyes wandered to the distant hills: further, wider and darker than the hills at home. She thought on the changing colours of her life's landscape. Fiery red sandstone, alive with troglodyte birds in the summer and glowing like a jewel in the sun swapped after the first twenty years for street after street of dominant red brick, factory built and rigid with work ethic, still haunted by hollow eyed children alongside their parents, if they were lucky, bent under the rod.

'What brings you to the Camino?'

Dominic snapped her back to the burnt ochre and the heat. The path was the colour of the little removable square in the paint box she had loved as a child with its unfathomable name printed beneath: gamboge. He wanted to know her story. She suspected he was after a drama or excitement, but her story was ordinary, an everyday tale of dysfunction.

'It's complicated.'

Dominic shifted his position so that he was turned towards her and settled in for the wait.

'I wouldn't know where to start.'

He rested her hand on his chest and put his over the top, a reassuring gesture, willing her to tell him.

29

She wondered if this was seduction. Were middle-aged Dutchmen interested in the lives of middle-aged English women? She felt overexposed at the thought of telling inner secrets to a near stranger and then bravura, who better than a stranger?

'Start at the beginning,' he said

There was sudden relief and she tried to dismiss the tide of emotions sweeping her to the brink of tears. She looked into the wide blue eyes. Perhaps she did not trust herself after all. The words that came surprised her and the crisis passed.

'It's as if my past is catching up with me.'

'Were you troublesome?' Dominic gave a knowing smile. He told her that he worked with disaffected youth, creating drama workshops. Perhaps he wanted tales of arson and disturbed behaviour.

'It has to do with my father, my life, everything.'

She told him how her father had disappeared when she was five years old. Her voice faltered at the sadness of the sentence. She hadn't known that it would and the self indulgence it conveyed annoyed her. She told him that the sudden absence had consumed her and filled her childhood with emptiness and longing that had never been voiced or discussed. Only as an adult had she realized the mistake of thinking children can be too young to grieve: it denies them the opportunity and the pain is internalised. That was the pattern of her life.

'Were you in trouble?' He asked her again.

'Did it make me a handful, do you mean? Did I grieve the loss? Did it break my heart with a wound a lifetime deep that gaped like a cruel smile and refused to heal?' *What ever would make you think that?*

He laughed, but she wasn't sure he had understood she wasn't really joking.

'Do you remember him?' Dominic wanted to

know. 'Did you never see him?'

He was probing for details so they would resurface like dead bodies in stagnant water. She knew exactly the little offering of memories and wasn't sure what effect speaking them aloud would have: a decent burial, perhaps.

'I have seen him and yes, I think I can remember quite a bit about him, enough to know we were better off without him.'

Dominic was stung. How could she could seriously think that? His family had been very loving, although very poor, and now he was a very loving father and a very important part of his children's lives.

'At least he didn't refuse all contact once we found him again,' Rosemary continued. 'I went to see him just before coming on the walk, the second time in forty years; one last attempt to understand. The visit was the catalyst for coming to the Camino.'

But it was not a chemical reaction, not even visceral; everything was too far gone for that. It was as if the thread holding her together had finally disintegrated.

'When I stood on his doorstep at the appointed hour he did not say hello, he asked me why I had come. *What have you come for?* Not angry, just mystified. He had no inkling. I think when he had closed the door on his wife and three children so many years ago he genuinely forgot our existence. It was as if we were snapshots and he had put us away in a cardboard box and sealed the lid. It was his next one liner that really did it.'

This time Dominic stayed quiet, just listening. She told Dominic what he had said.

For God's sake don't tell anyone who you are.

Even saying the words again out loud she felt

31

them echo, bouncing off the empty sky and it was almost as if her husband, Seb, was speaking them. Her life was based on the false premise that she had been loved all along. She groped towards the reason why she had felt so utterly miserable as if someone, suddenly and briefly had switched on a light, then just as suddenly, switched it off.

'What did you say to your father?'

'Well, nothing.'

'Weren't you angry?'

Anger had crackled through her like electricity before a storm, followed by the familiar heart failing sense of futility, abrupt as the needle snatched off a favourite tune: a tune only ever imagined. She had felt the impotence of rage. To awaken after the long sleepwalk of life and still be in the dark. It was not the rage that made for impotence, but the other way about. There is no way to counteract a bully. All remonstration is pointless because that, too, is delicious to the bully.

'I understood how he must have felt to have his past still taunt him. At nearly eighty perhaps you've earned the right for your past to lie down and die.'

Dominic's voice was suddenly raised and forceful in the stillness of the plain, 'That is a terrible thing to say to a person. You should have said something.'

She felt a clicking like the release of a tight coil and was aware of Dominic watching her. He put his arm around her and gave her a squeeze. His tone brightened as if to change the subject.

'Let's get walking. It's time for a coffee, maybe we are nearly at the town.'

She watched him toss his rucksack carelessly on his back, before slowly, painfully struggling each arm into the straps of her own.

'Is there nothing in your rucksack?' she asked

32

'It weighs about ten percent of body weight, as recommended.'

'Oh.' Hers was probably thirty percent. No wonder it felt heavy. Dominic took her hand in his.

'It will be all right, you know.'

The comfort of his concern made her want to cry. She wasn't sure what he meant and that also made her want to cry. They were silent for a while as they concentrated on the rhythm of moving together.

'My father was a tailor. I remember him sitting cross-legged on the table by the window, for the light. He worked hard for his family, too hard.'

'Was he tall, Dominic, like you?' hard to imagine someone of Dominic's height cross-legged on a table. She had interrupted his story.

'No, he was small. There wasn't enough food in the war for him to grow tall. His sons and daughters are tall, though. He was my role model, but he died too young, of a heart attack when I was only thirteen. His father too had died that way.'

Perhaps, for a child, death was a more respectable absence than desertion, though no less painful. She thought of fairy stories with hard working tailors and thought of her own childhood. Perhaps her sister was her role model. She had certainly looked to her for advice and approval. She looked at Dominic, lost in thought. He was, she supposed, reassessing the main tenets of his life: family, love, work.

'And your wife?'

'We are not married. Janneka is the mother of my children and I love her. We did not promise fidelity, just love.'

She felt threatened; the bloody Dutch are so liberal, such free thinkers.

'I have been married to one man for twenty six
33

years.'

Dominic was incredulous that anyone could be faithful for twenty-six years. He whistled repeating twenty-six years, trying to imagine it.

'It's not that unusual, Dominic.'

Not in the quiet suburbs she had left behind. Not in the huge parish where they went to Mass week after week without ever getting to know anyone. Perhaps Dominic was right to be incredulous that anyone could stay married. Perhaps she was one of those invisible women whose identity becomes a blur, a pale reflection of her husband, over long years of marriage. The words of a song that she remembered sung huskily by George Moustaki, that she had sung in her youth and thought desperately romantic, no longer seemed anything to sing about.

Je ne sais pas ou tu commences, tu ne sais pas ou je fini.

It had seemed as neat as a helix: I don't know where you start; you don't know where I end; it was tortuous as a knotted snake.

They could hear the rumble of traffic, the zoom of a motorbike. Wild flowers and grass along the path were replaced by a broken sink and a pile of rubble that included glass, several empty bottles and a splatter of used condoms. Ahead, a high arching bridge spanned a river and a small town was waking to a day of commerce and order. Life's excess and that of the night before left out of sight on an old byway. Dominic consulted her watch, reaching for her wrist with his free hand; he never liked to wear one, he said. They had walked a distance of some eight kilometres in less than an hour.

'That's fast. That's really fast. We have done well together.' Dominic made a low whistle.

'You are the Flying Dutchman,' she wanted to praise him and he was charmed by the epithet.

34

FIVE

They had coffee in a small café still rubbish-strewn and dirty from the night before. Dominic grumbled about the mess but that did not stop him adding to it. He tossed the skin of a banana he had just eaten onto the sawdust on the floor. No one noticed, no one cared.

The angry young man from the night before came into the café just as they were about to leave. Dominic greeted him like an old friend with manly hugs and slaps on the back.

'This is Stefan.'

She smiled, 'Hello Stefan; we met yesterday, I think.'

Stefan did not acknowledge her. He was grumbling, his blisters, his boots, nothing was right. He had not even walked that morning and had hired a taxi to bring him to this town but the fare had been extortionate, the ride uncomfortable. His grumbling filled the café and drew glances from the few quiet businessmen slowly stirring their coffee at the bar who had been concentrating on their newspapers. The young girl behind the bar, uncertain what to make of this young man, was less discreet and made no pretence of staring. Her mouth was hanging open as if she had simply forgotten to close it. She was at that awkward stage of adolescence: disproportionate and spotty. A girl from such a place, whose options for life resembled those of a goldfish; a small glass bubble from which she could look out, imagine, but never escape, must wonder what life is like for an outsider. The girl closed her mouth and opened it again with a slight pop when a voice that could have been her mother's shouted from behind a bead curtain. She disappeared through the curtain with a toss of her head. The clicking of the beads and their slight sway was the only testament to her existence.

Stefan threw his rucksack on a chair with a chink of glass from jars or bottles. He sprawled in another, calling for a cup of coffee, and some toast. He put one foot up next to his rucksack keeping it in agitated, perpetual motion. An angry, red welt striped down the side of his leg.

'You need some suntan lotion,' Rosemary said absently and he glared at her. She handed him the large bottle from her bag, 'Help me use it up, it's heavy.'

His smile transformed him and lit up the café. An aura of menace that had set the place on edge evaporated and his 'thanks very much,' sounded genuine.

Stefan and Dominic had much to talk about: films, politics, travel. She was not expected to join in although not intentionally excluded. Their heads were close and they laughed like schoolboys, willing each other to daredevil exploits or to say something outrageous. It crossed her mind that both were showing off. After a while she grew tired of sitting still and watching them.

'I think I'll set off.'

Stefan tapped his cigarette box on the table and raised one eyebrow to look at her, 'We'll catch you up. Don't go too fast.'

The rucksack was heavier than ever and she hauled herself to her feet.

'See you soon then.'

It was strange, saying that as if they were the oldest of friends when really they had only just met, like ships merely dipping ensigns. But how else were friendships formed? There must be a moment when you know nothing of another person and a moment when you decide that you would like to know more. At the doorway she turned back and saw them still lost in conversation before she lunged into the street.

People were making their way to their offices, shops, banks in a steady stream that was difficult to cut across with her load and she missed her footing. She did not fall immediately, but seemed to travel through the air in a glorious arc several feet from where she had taken off. The inevitable impact was heavy and she smacked her face hard on the pavement. Blood filled her mouth with a taste of iron and two bright red spots appeared on the pavement beneath her. Silent, violent splashes, incongruous as images in a Buñuel film.

Ay! La pobre. Poor thing

She sat stunned with her head in her hands staring at smart shoes that had formed a circle round her. Soon, hands were helping her to her feet and there was laughter and the word *peregrina,* pilgrim, repeated over and over.

'That was spectacular.'

Dominic looked down at her. Even with the throb of her cheek bone and the pain where her teeth had cut her tongue she was impressed by the way sunlight framed his head, playing tricks with his hair till it stood out like a halo. Encased in black with the sun behind him she thought he was a fallen angel.

Stefan stood nearby, nonchalantly smoking. 'You've already got a bruise coming,' he said and passed her a hanky.

'Thanks.' She was inordinately impressed, not by the gesture, but by the beautiful laundering of the hanky.

'Do you want to go back to the café? Get some

37

water or something?'

Dominic took her hand and led her the short way back.

Inside was almost empty. The businessmen had gone to work; the young girl was lolling on the counter flicking through a magazine. She ignored Rosemary as successfully as she ignored the shouted instructions from her mother from behind the bead curtain. She was supposed to be clearing up, taking advantage of the lull between customers to sweep away the remains from the night before. Little screws of paper, cocktail sticks and cigarette butts still littered the floor, wet rings from glasses glistened on tables in the dark interior as sunlight caught them.

Rosemary left the door of the communal lavatory ajar, splashed her face with cold water from the stained basin and squinted into a mirror so mottled that the reflection did not look like her at all. She could not see the graze and large bruise on her cheek or the swelling of her lip, although she could feel them acutely. She ran cold water through Stefan's hanky and laid it alternately on her cheek and her lip, pressing gently till the cold penetrated. She no longer felt like rushing off on her own.

Dominic and Stefan waited for her outside in the street. Dominic continued where he had left off as if there had not been a slight hiccough to their conversation.

'It's all right for you, a young man, with your life ahead. I'm nearly fifty and it's a last adventure.'

Stefan grimaced, threw his cigarette to the ground, watching the curling smoke and said quietly, 'Nothing's all right for me, Dominic.'

Dominic was used to being listened to and did not register Stefan's reaction or his reply.

38

'Well it's not quite my last adventure. I might lose some weight maybe, a few love affairs.'

Stefan nodded his head towards the door of the bar through which Rosemary had disappeared. 'You're wasting your time here.'

'I never waste my time, Stefan, and I like a challenge.'

He eyed Stefan and thought how disappointed he looked for a man with the grace of youth and rude health. Life is needlessly complicated for some.

'So what *is* eating you?'

Stefan glared at his boots accusingly, but blisters were the least of his problems. How to explain the worm that rotted his entrails? Jealousy? Fear of failure? Not the mere fear; the reality. It stared him in the face; it stared back at him in the morning and taunted him at noon it kept him awake at night. He grinned at Dominic, nodding to the doorway of the café.

'Here she is then.'

When Rosemary joined them, looking a little pale, Dominic took her hand and gave it a gentle squeeze. 'Better?' She nodded.

They set off together in a line filling the pavement. Dominic held Rosemary's hand and Stefan marched beside her.

'You two look like an old married couple, a large bruise the size of a fist on her face and holding hands to make up.' Stefan said.

Dominic laughed, but Rosemary was appalled. She was slightly relieved when Stefan made an excuse not to walk with them. He wanted to make phone calls he said and at last he had a signal. His mobile rarely worked in these Godforsaken villages. He did want to know where they were headed for the night so they could meet up. Dominic knew exactly and reeled off the name of a distant village. She was highly sceptical and managed a low whistle; the distance seemed too ambitious, especially in her present state.

'That's about thirty kilometres from here. I hadn't intended to walk so far today.' Before she could continue with her argument for a shorter day Dominic replied, 'We'll both be there.'

Dominic held Stefan's gaze then turned and began to walk away leading Rosemary by the hand.

She could have argued, but somehow it didn't matter that the Dutchman answered for her. She would like to push herself and see if she could walk the distance; she would like to walk with Dominic.

Small, elegant gold studs embedded in the pavement marked the route.

SIX

They came to the old bridge where the stones had been worn smooth by the passing of feet over many years. Houses several stories high curved down to the banks on either side of the river.

'I think I will give up everything,' Dominic said, 'Buy a little place on the Camino; make coffee for pilgrims. What about you? Would you like to do that?'

'No, I'd rather die outright,' Rosemary did not hesitate, 'like being buried alive.'

Dominic pulled a face at her and laughed.

'Live a clean, simple life. Look at this place it has nothing, but I bet people are happy.'

'I doubt it. Look at the young girl in the café; she has no life, no prospects to speak of, just wistful dreams and narrow horizons.'

'What girl?' Dominic said without looking at her.

'There, that's what I mean. You didn't even notice her.'

'Do you mean the lazy, sulky teenager? She would be lazy and sulky wherever she was.'

'Maybe,' Rosemary said. The memory of being a lazy, sulky teenager was vivid. Time was elastic and she saw herself as she used to stand in front of a mirror; aware of her reflected self diminishing into the future. Dominic would not have noticed *her* either.

'I'm too old anyway.'

Dominic clicked his tongue. 'Don't say that. It means I am too old too.'

'I'm a whole year older don't forget. Besides you're a bloke; the world's your oyster.'

'We say that too, in Holland; the world is full of

hidden treasures.'

'Perhaps I just don't look hard enough. What were you like as a teenager?'

'Tall, but not lazy; I can't remember. Too much has happened since.'

The path stretched out like a long yellow scar through endless stubble fields disappearing into the heat. Sunshine was burning one leg and one arm because they were heading due west; side by side with Dominic. There was a hard climb to reach a plain of endless vines: Rioja region. They stopped in the dust in mid path. The sky, a huge, blue dome arching over them, they lolled on rucksacks and drank sun-warm water. Dominic's gentle voice lilted in the emptiness of the plain. They were the only two people in that world. He touched the large bruise on her face, turning her chin up to see the extent of it. She had almost forgotten.

'Does your husband beat you?'

'Certainly not.'

He nodded and took hold of her hand; small in his, opening out his fingers to show how much longer they were than hers.

'Cool hands, Dominic.' He roared with laughter,

'You know what they say. Cool hands, warm heart.'

'Yes, yes.'

But his laughter was infectious and it was so good to laugh.

They had a picnic lunch in a village square: bread and oily tuna from a tin that a kitten was desperate to share. Rosemary placed the tin under the bench and watched the neat little mouth dip into it.

There were others enjoying the shade in the square: two immaculately dressed children with their grandfather. The old chap, who looked as if he was recovering from a stroke, was taking his constitutional, up and down, painfully slowly with the help of a Zimmer frame and the encouragement of the children. It was not obvious who was looking after whom; the two generations worked together in symbiosis. The old man encouraged the children to great exploits on their stabilized bicycles. Every time they racketed round a corner and were in danger of tipping, he would call out, *Eso, eso*. That's the way.

They would wait for him to catch up, turning to look over a shoulder to watch him and speeding off when he was on the point of doing so.

'*Vale Abuelo, Vale,*' ok, granddad, ok.

A cry they had overheard at football matches with their father or perhaps at a bullfight or even in the playground.

The old man stopped every time he drew near Dominic and Rosemary, relaxed on their bench and, seeing they were foreigners, commented on different places of interest, pointing a wavering finger to the horizon. The heat was soporific even in the shade. The plastic bottle of water in Rosemary's hand was fit to melt and she considered the effort of walking a few meters to the town fountain. The old man nodded at the bottle and rolled his eyes towards the fountain: the water always so pure and so cold, straight from the mountains. Again, the sepia hand left the safety of the walking frame and he kissed his fingers to the fountain in praise of its water. Rosemary went to taste it. A steady trickle from a pipe emerged from a granite block. '*Eso, eso.*' the old man cried, but Rosemary could not be sure if he was pleased that she had taken his advice or if he was simply praising his grandchildren.

43

They walked, brisk and far, hand in hand amid fields of vines, painful shoulders and painful feet alternately troublesome or forgotten. Two dots in a vast landscape, distant hum of tractors, sweat beading on Dominic's face, his bright hair dancing to the rhythm of his feet. Her bruise throbbed. A high, distant village overlooked the fields.

'That is where we are going,'

'There's no hostel mentioned in my book.'

'Believe me, it's there.' A friend had told him about it, he said.

'What about Stefan? He will be expecting to see you.'

'He won't be too surprised, I don't think.'

Air was too hot to breathe and still they walked through rows of vines so neat and so new, they reminded her of hair parted into tiny plaits. The village grew slowly larger as if they were drawing it nearer to them on a secret thread. Finally, Dominic led Rosemary between close houses winding up in tight circles. He stopped outside a converted barn and banged on the huge door.

'This is it.'

Rosemary was too thirsty to ask how ever had he found it.

A young man answered, opening just a tiny section, and bid them enter a stone flagged covered yard.

'*Mi casa es tu casa,*' he said with a smile surprisingly full of gold teeth in one so young. He stood back to allow them to pass into the cool entrance.

He showed them the hostel leading them up three flights and through three floors full of bunks. It looked newly converted. There was no one else there.

'Anywhere you like,' the young man said, leaving

them on the top floor.

Dominic led the way back down.

'Here is my bed.'

He had chosen a bottom bunk in a dark corner of the room, almost a recess. There was an adjacent bunk but Rosemary moved away a little and chose a top bunk where she could see out of the window when she woke up. She climbed up and sat with her legs dangling, trying it out. He came and stood beside her, putting his arms either side of her legs, and she shivered.

'You are a little bit afraid of the Flying Dutchman?'

'Not afraid, exactly.'

'Is it sex that frightens you, then?'

She did not reply. For a moment she was tempted to laugh and she had to concentrate to keep a straight face. She was tempted to rail, *I was educated in convents all my life, went from an all female household straight in to marriage. Give me a break,* but her throat constricted the words.

She wondered if he had ever read *Dangerous Liaisons, Les Liaisons Dangereuses,* one of the French texts studied at university and hotly discussed in tutorials, tales of innocence led astray.

Dominic did not insist on an answer. He took her face gently in his hands and kissed her slowly, deliberately, sweetly: a text book kiss.

'Not so frightening?'

'You just don't understand.'

'Try me.'

'You think one night with a stranger will solve everything.'

'It would go a long way, yes.' He would have kissed her again.

'I didn't come to the Camino looking for

45

complications.'

'Just lucky, then?' He ruffled her hair as he would a child or pet.

She could have hit him. Dominic put his hands in front of him defensively. 'Ok, ok.'

There was a patio overlooking fields with row after row of vines. A distant buzz came from a tiny tractor down amongst them and huge winged birds circled overhead. The late afternoon sun was still hot and Dominic was tired and sensibly wanted to rest. He sat on one of the upright chairs, stretched his long legs and let his chin relax on his chest, instantly asleep like a child. Rosemary wanted to explore, speak some Spanish and be sure of provisions for the following day for her and for Dominic. He paid no heed to minor details like feeding himself. No doubt Janneka, the mother of his children to whom he was not married, took care of it.

The village was sleepy, the doors and shutters closed against the heat of the day; or against marauding foreigners. Sometimes shops looked like living rooms and had such meagre provisions it felt an imposition to buy their produce, as if it were denying locals of the chance. When she finally found the *ultramarinos*, the grocery, the dark musty interior was deserted, but as she was eyeing the wrinkled apples La Señora stirred from the back, smiling toothlessly and as wizened as the fruit, but willing to part with it.

SEVEN

Stefan slumped in a pavement café drinking coffee and nursing his blisters. He took out his phone blinking in mock disbelief at the sign indicating a good signal. He scoffed. No messages. Again. He was hoping for some word from the film institute. He knew there would be nothing else, although he had not given up looking. Morning noon and night, he checked, just in case, with the usual mix of anger and despair. Then he punched in his own thrice-daily message: not a new message; it said simply, 'Thinking of you,' which he was with every breath he took, but it was getting better. His finger ached to press send and he let it go slack. Instead he saved it with all his other messages to her.

He ordered another coffee, taking a moment to scan the tables. There were a few pilgrims in ill-assorted clothes and headscarves; the sight of their earnest faces revolted him. There was also a rather attractive woman who appeared to be staring at him. He wondered if she was a bottle blonde; her hair looked good and blonde curls were his favourite. He tried to soften the sardonic smile he knew twisted his lips these days; he wanted to make a good impression. She actually winked. He gulped too much coffee, burned his mouth and put his cup down with a clatter and she laughed. He winced.

'*Enfant sauvage, que tu es beau!*'

He wasn't sure what she had said to him, but her voice purred and he liked the sound.

'*Viens, viens,*' and she beckoned.

He did not need a second invitation.

'Do you speak German?' She shook her head. 'English?' She shook her head. 'Ah well.'

47

Close up she was even more beautiful than he had thought, but much older. Her skin looked polished and her perfume filled the morning. Her long slim hands were covered in a delicate tracery of veins. She had a newspaper in front of her folded neatly at the crossword. None of the clues had been filled in although here and there, little balloons of words unravelled waiting to provide answers.

As he sat down his bag knocked the table spilling a little of her coffee. She snatched up the paper to save it from damage and revealed a drawing underneath, a pencil sketch, which she also saved from the spill. Having apologised for his clumsiness Stefan asked permission to look at the drawing, holding out his hand and smiling. He raised an eyebrow when he realised that the sketch was of him and not a bad likeness; he studied her questioningly. He was disconcerted that he had been observed without his being aware.

She shrugged; there was no way to explain that it was the expression on his face that she had wanted to capture: an expression that altered his face as utterly as catastrophic storms break the sky; a change that she found beautiful. She would like to smooth the furrow between his eyes before it became ugly and permanent, as she would correct a mistake on a statue, kneading with fingers slick with slip and water. She imagined the feel of his skin as if it were stone in her hands; warm with possibilities where the sun rested on it and cold and barren where it did not. She could just reach forward with her hand and close his jaw that he had left open. She felt almost tenderly for this young man and realised with a wry smile the feeling was maternal.

She was aware Stefan was still staring and his look was not filial. She was accustomed to that look; she

48

should move on. She had often wondered if, had she not been beautiful, she would have become an artist. It was as if the constant praise for her appearance— which really was not of her doing—prompted her to seek recognition for something worthier.

She thought of her quirky statues, obscene some called them, that peopled private and public spaces and were now highly sought after. Giant bronze genitals, large enough for children to play on; recumbent nudes whose splayed limbs and intimate places provided shelter for outdoor theatre goers; a large dog that took its owner for a walk and appeared to tug the lead so that the owner could not relieve himself: each unique and shocking. An intriguing view of the world; humorous; playful observations that mock preconceptions: just some of her reviews. But it was not for accolades; it was simply for the anarchic joy.

Stefan closed his mouth and swallowed hard. He gazed back to the drawing in his hands: she had captured his ugly smile perfectly. He felt a lump rise in his throat and that pricking behind his eyes. The drawing was signed *Murielle*, written in French script with a line under it. He thought it might be easy to forge signatures in France since everyone's writing was the same.

'Murielle?' he said running his finger below the name. She nodded, then gestured that he could keep the picture.

'*Merci*,' and he smiled his lopsided half smile.

She picked up her small bag, left a few coins for her coffee and, with a shrug and '*Au revoir*' was gone. He had not even told her his name, but when he looked there was no sign of her.

He discovered another page of sketches of an octagonal church underneath the one she had given him that he was sure she had not meant to give away. He recognised it. He had also made the small detour through fields to the Knights Templar church at Eunate. He had wanted to see how light would look in a turret that was lined with abalone. He had not been disappointed, but he had not been as impressed as Murielle. The sketches were minutely detailed and he was tempted to go back and look with fresh eyes.

Stefan tested his feet on the hard pavement and limped into the bar to phone for a taxi. Common sense would tell anyone with blisters like his that walking thirty kilometres was not an option, but he really did want to speak to Dominic. He held the coin for the phone in his hand, deliberating. He did not want to cheat and yet he had not counted on blisters. As he dialled and inserted his coin, he decided he would get the taxi to drop him off some kilometres before the agreed destination so he could still meet Dominic and only have to walk a short way. He felt pleased with this compromise; it would fulfil his obligation, his self imposed obligation to walk just a hundred kilometres which was the minimum distance required in order to obtain an indulgence. That always made him smile: a plenary indulgence from the church—the mean-minded, unforgiving church. It was not a concrete thing you could touch either. It was on account; it meant dispensation from the long years to be spent in purgatory. What difference to eternity would ten years make? He could never understand why people were so trusting. He envied them their faith, although he believed it to be the result of a narrow, untutored mind. Surely anyone with half a brain could see the church for what it was—a corrupt institution living in opulence off the backs of the faithful. Come to think of it that description could apply to almost any large organisation. Still, only the church offered indulgences and he wanted one.

'*Hola. Hola. Si, Taxi, por favor.*'

'*Taxi no hay. No more taxi.*'

Murielle stopped on her way out of the small town to take photographs of the ancient bridge that gave the town its name, Puente La Reina, now just a footbridge and long since usurped by a concrete one strong enough to take heavy traffic. It had been built for pilgrims by Queen Urraca, daughter of Alfonso VI, the self appointed Emperor of all the Iberian Peninsula and a great Christian King, so that they could cross the gorge in safety without having to negotiate the torrential waters below. The bridge was almost pink in the sunlight and worth photographing; maybe she could do something with the pictures when she got home. She lingered on the bridge expecting to see marvels and for a moment felt time suspended. One intake of breath connected her with past and future pilgrims, but on the out breath she saw that the raging torrent had dwindled to a trickle that merely wetted the white stone of the riverbed. Civic pride that had led the inhabitants to build such a splendid bridge had dwindled too; the banks way below were squalid with rubbish.

She had studied her itinerary well; cherry picked her destinations and researched buses and taxis before setting out. Public transport was surprisingly good and frequent for such obscure places. She knew when to walk and when to ride. This bridge had been on her to-see list. She was gathering material for one last exhibition, although the plan was not clear. This morning there had been the surprise of the angry young man. She liked the way life threw up unexpected leads.

When Murielle told the hospital that she would be away for a while to walk the Camino, the nurses thought it was a beautiful thing for anyone to do. (They mean, anyone in my circumstances, Murielle had told herself.) Her doctor, of a more practical bent, had advised her not to go, but knowing that Murielle did not take advice readily, he'd added, 'As your friend I wish you good luck and give you this. I think you will need both.'

He had written a name and contact details on a prescription pad as if prescribing medicine, torn it from the pad and handed it to her. He knew a man, an old friend of his father's, he said, a Spaniard and a priest who was a *hospitalero*, almost an old fashioned almoner, who ministered all summer to pilgrims under his roof. He would look after her when the time came.

She had never thought of mortality, until it stared her in the face. Tests; results; more tests; disbelief and pain; she even began to wonder if a worldview such as hers had induced illness. Desire to shock had deserted her and she was wretched but determined. The determination had helped her walk so much of the Camino; the wretchedness returned as her strength began to fail.

'Just don't push yourself,' her partner, Jacques, had said.

'What sort of a life is that?' She'd asked him but he had no answer.

'I will contact you when I am ready.' She'd said and he had accepted her terms as he accepted all the others, with resignation.

'You never let me in,' he had tried to complain and she had stopped him. She had not asked him to love her.

52

She was weary. Perhaps if she rested beside the path the young man from the morning would just happen on her and they could walk together. It started to drizzle and Murielle turned her face up to enjoy the sensation. A dog began to howl, soon joined by others, till the sound was of wolves taking on collective pain, echoing off the bare hills and bringing the sky down to the ground in tears. A Russian sound from the Steppes, from a desolate place one hopes only to visit in dreams or the depths of a sleepless night at its darkest and coldest. A place glimpsed in unguarded moments behind the eyes of someone loosing their mind: an enormous black void filled with the howling of wolves. She had not expected to find emptiness here. She had thought of entering noisy rooms and sleeping with the masses, scratching with their flees, suffering their smells and night noises, simply to know she was still alive.

When the drizzle turned to rain Murielle cut her losses and went to get the bus.

EIGHT

When they were going out to eat that evening Dominic bought Rosemary a pendant in the shape of a yellow arrow that the owner of the hostel had made and hung it round her neck. She was surprised by the gesture and felt called on to buy him one, with a mixed feeling of guilt and pleasure.

'We are good together,' he said and smiled.

He sat down like an obedient child so that she could fasten it. She made him bend his head forward and smoothed his hair away from his neck. It was slightly damp. When the clasp was fastened she rested her fingers briefly on his brown neck, warm under her cool fingers. Then she lightly tugged on a small strand of his hair to let him know that he could look up. His long slim fingers reached for hers. She did not complain. He assumed that she would like to hold hands and she did; it felt affectionate and reminded her of all the little hands slipped into hers. At first, the tiny grip able only to grasp a finger as if clinging to life itself. Then, the dimpled hands, reaching for reassurance as much for her as for themselves, sometimes collecting all three children, one held simply by pressure of thumb. She and Seb hardly ever held hands and when she commented on this one time, Seb had said he thought it was something she did not like doing; at least that is what she had said at eighteen, saying it as if the memory of the snub still caused him pain. She could not recall ever having said that. She had felt like shaking him. *For god's sake, we're nearly fifty, now.*

The meal was intimate, even though the room of the only tavern was brisk with locals. No one took any notice of them as if they were visible only to each other. Their cheeks were glowing after three courses, a flagon of red wine and the day's exertions.

'I thought I would stay in a quiet village again tomorrow night,' Rosemary said.

'No, the next town is our destination, Santo Domingo, named for me especially. You must stay with me, of course.'

She was growing accustomed to this presumption. It was as if he had planned to find a woman to walk with, for whom he would buy a pendant of the yellow arrow and with whom he would arrive in the town with his name. She was the one chancing along acting out a bit part in his story with no story of her own. Her head was too hot to dwell on so sobering a thought, so she brushed it aside, knowing as she did that it was a pattern repeated often.

Dominic spoke of love.

'My mother has a lover.'

She could have said, 'My mother does not—not after the first.' But that might have spoiled a story that she sensed was coming.

'She has been many years on her own after my father died and she was so lonely, I think. It is not good to live without love. Now when I speak to her she tells me of warm nights and her body excited by the sound of her new man's voice.'

Rosemary could think of nothing to say. Her mind was full of images, love scenes in Technicolor films, but no words. Talking of sex in a room full of strangers they would never see again, who possibly did not even see them, was disturbing. She could not think of any intimate friends or brief acquaintances with whom the topic of conversation would be the sex life of one of their parents. Prudish? Very probably, English, certainly. She thought of the arguing pilgrims on the first night and of national

55

stereotypes. Did Dominic want to make her weak at the knees with his talk or was he just being Dutch? She felt one of them was missing a vital point.

They had the hostel to themselves. Dominic stood by her bunk. 'So,' he said. As Rosemary turned in the half dark the black patch of window was bright with stars and she was distracted like a child.

'Look at that. I knew this was a good place, you can see shooting stars from here.'

She led him to the window and opened it. Crickets were still singing, the air was warm and somewhere beneath them was the enclosed sound of revellers in the tavern. The pattern of their vines, the fruit of their labours, laid out hopefully in the good earth below. Dominic stood close to her and murmured, 'The night smells so good. Jasmine, maybe.'

It was a scent for lovers: heady and intoxicating with the power of oblivion.

'Don't you feel it?' Dominic asked and brushed his lips behind her ear.

She assumed he meant the stirring of passion, that quickening of pulse and shortness of breath, as if someone has sucked the air out of you. Yes, there was all that. She might have liked to be a heroine who could swoon in the arms of her hero with no thought for consequences, but her head always ruled. It wasn't simply fear of life, although that played a part. There was also yearning: a sense of loss so keen it overrode all else, as if year by year, little by little she had given herself away till she was hollow and any stranger could claim squatters rights or say, *Don't tell anyone who you are.* Besides. She was not impervious; only her heart was cold as tungsten steel. A shard of ice had lodged there since childhood and despite the best attempts of her mother and sisters, even her husband and children, it would not dislodge. He must know the story? So the quick fix he was proposing not only would be useless, it was potentially damaging for him.

Harsh sounds of bikes and padlocks and cursing came from the street. A bell clanged and half a dozen cyclists came tramping up steps, banging doors behind them.

'Saved by the bell,' Rosemary said and Dominic laughed. She felt she should say more than just goodnight.

'There is the sort of man a mother would like her daughter to marry; we say that he is a one-gal-guy. Well, I'm a one-guy-gal.'

Dominic's eyes had already glazed over and he turned to get into bed. She imagined disappointment, but then he was asleep and snuffling gently almost as his head touched the pillow.

Wine coursed her veins and she could not quiet her mind after the long day, the unaccustomed talk and shattered stillness. As she felt her eyes closing she noticed a large spider on the ceiling, but by then was too drowsy to move. A cool breeze blew through her dreams carrying whispered words: *promiscuous promiscuous*. A hammer bludgeoned a large bell and three words rang out: *one gal guy*.

She woke; some small sound magnified by the night; a spider dropping on her sleeping bag from a great height and she jumped out of the top bunk in the dark with dread. She went and sat in the kitchen with a cup of tea till the spider had gone and thought hard of her marriage vows. How comforting it was to sleep beside Seb. How easy would it be to lie beside Dominic and sleep with his arms round her? She thought of Klimt's lovers kissing; of their golden, undulating bed adorned with flowers and the expression of bliss on the face of the young woman. She imagined hot, urgent lips and the warmth of hot breath in her hair and felt the familiar tide that swept her along, hurtling aside everything in its path; the inexorable tide of her life over which she wanted to take control.

The refrain of a tango song drifted in to her head, *un jardin de illusion*, a garden of illusion. She hummed the tune, filling in words as they came. *tus ojos de enigma bordado*, your eyes veiled in enigma. She didn't know them all. It was the sound of the words from the throaty voice in the recording she liked. A new night class; frivolous, she had sensed Seb's disdain. She stood up with her eyes closed to practise *ochos*, forward and back figures of eight, sliding her feet along the floor in their sensible sandals. 'You must be like cats slinking their paws,' their tango teacher said, 'Maybe I will make you keep pieces of paper sliding under your feet.' She swayed as the moon scattered its silver particles through the hostel till she was ready for sleep.

NINE

Stefan found that by cursing aloud and counting on alternate steps he could actually make progress.

'One fuck, two fuck, three fuck, four...'

There was no one else there and besides it amused him. He laughed aloud that he was counting fucks not steps and it occurred that perhaps he was keeping score for Dominic and the chant ceased to amuse him and his blisters chafed all the more. Damn and blast. He threw his bag to the ground and reached in his shirt pocket for his light meter. It was cool in his fingers, a small thing. A prism that rose tinted the day better than any hallucinogen. He squatted at the side of the road to get a better perspective and felt the skin of his calves stretch where the sun had burned. The sun was fierce on his head after a spattering of rain had come to nothing. He replaced his light meter lovingly and took out his mobile to punch in his meaningless message. He knew his feelings were not reciprocated; he knew she did not miss him. When that thought did not make him angry it made him sad and that was worse than feeling angry.

The bus station, little more than a dust bowl beside the main road, had a cafeteria with a decent menu. 'There is a God.' Stefan laughed at his good fortune. He threw his bag on one chair and himself into another in his usual fashion. He tried to catch the attention of the bartender, a small man, half hidden behind the bar. The bartender carried on slowly washing up glasses at a low sink, only occasionally looking up and then only looking to the middle distance. Stefan thought this was deliberate and was because he was so obviously a foreigner. He came and stood at the bar prepared for a fight. The man immediately dried his hands and asked what he could get for him. Stefan was soothed and realised he had been mistaken. The bartender suggested a meal, gesturing with his head to the separate dining room.

The meal was splendid; suckling pig, palely gold and unctuous and Stefan, feeling lavish, treated himself to brandy with his coffee. The Spanish knew how to live: simply but well. He was surprised how many people had sat in the cool dining room with white tablecloths to be served by a motherly looking woman and a raven-haired beauty and not one of them gave any indication they thought the excellence of the meal and the service was anything unusual. He looked at his watch. His fingers twitched to write a message; there would be time before the bus arrived. He felt the old urge to send all the saved messages, one after the other, to arrive like a plague in her inbox, and ordered another brandy. He could sleep on the bus and ask the driver to warn him when to get off. It would be good to talk to Dominic; it would be good to have his advice.

Stefan's eyes were heavy with the motion of the bus and he leaned his head against the tinted glass that kept the heat of the sun out. As he was finishing his meal there had been a heavy downpour and the sun had not yet reclaimed its rightful place. The air conditioning made him feel chilly and he considered reaching a jumper out of his bag, but the brandy coursing his veins induced lethargy and a feeling of glowing akin to warmth. The bus jolted to a halt and the squeak of doors grated. A voice purred in his ear,

'*Ca ne te dérange pas trop?*'

Did she ask if she was bothering him? He had a vision of loveliness, of blonde curls and soft curves beside him. It was the familiar perfume that finally made him open his eyes.

'Murielle.'

She smiled a perfect smile, small pearly teeth and a mouth pretty enough to kiss. He sat up and rubbed a hand over his stubbly chin and felt unworthy, but finally awake. He told her he had her drawings and she did not understand. He told her that she was very beautiful and that he would like to fall in love with her and solve all his troubles, but still she did not understand. Both closed their eyes and dozed.

The next Stefan knew, the bus driver was calling him to get off. The bus had halted at a distant restaurant and several passengers stood outside smoking. Murielle was no longer beside him and he wondered if he had merely dreamt of her. He half staggered down the bus clutching his bag to his chest. The renewed pain in his feet made walking almost impossible.

A warm breeze blew as he descended the steps, but there was no sign of Murielle. He smoked a cigarette, anonymous in the circle of other passengers, recognising the occasional word of their intimate conversations. He ground the stub into the dust and limped off in the direction of the village Dominic had named. He left off his cursing and counting and simply trudged along the side of the road. The bus overtook him and he was sure he saw Murielle's face at the back window, turned to look at him, till the bus diminished into the distance.

When Stefan finally arrived at the hostel agreed by Dominic, his head was thick with too much brandy drunk too early in the day and his mouth was dry as dust from the journey. His feet throbbed in his boots after barely an hour's walk. He scanned the list of pilgrims already registered. Dominic's name was not there; neither was Rosemary's. Heat surged through his body like a pain and he wanted to destroy the register, rip out pages and hurl them across the floor. Dominic had been so certain. Why send him on a wild goose chase? Why not just say?

Then he noticed Murielle's name and beside it her age: 43. That morning she had looked a hundred. The anger he had felt was cooled and he was impelled to laugh; a dry impish laugh. He moved his hand away from his forehead where he rubbed absently and reached for his breast pocket to feel for his small round light meter and then moved to touch the hard outline of his phone. He grimaced and checked himself. Anyone seeing him might think he had a nervous tick or that he was making a sign of the cross.

There was a huge pile of boots at the foot of the stairs and he wondered briefly what had happened to the owners. He was about to climb the stairs to look for a place to lay his sleeping bag when a small woman appeared out of nowhere on silent slippers and rushed him with a broom. She started beating his legs and at first it did not hurt and he was consumed with laughter. When the beating got harder and his laughter subsided he caught the broom handle and tried to force it from her. She was tenacious and he grew flustered with the effort and the absurdity.

It was Murielle who rescued him, calmly speaking to the woman in French she obviously understood. The little woman took back her broom, smoothed her apron, scowled at Stefan and scurried away.

Murielle pointed to Stefan's boots. He gathered that they were the offending article, but did not relish losing them in the pile, however badly they chafed. She mimed a person taking off their boots and

62

carrying them close to the chest. Stefan copied her and when he had his boots in his hand, Murielle took his arm and escorted him up stairs where small rooms without doors were pressed full of bunks piled three high. Murielle invited him to sleep on a bottom bunk adjacent to hers, putting her delicate hands together on one cheek and inclining her head, as one would mime sleep to a child. Stefan staked his claim, placing his boots under his bed and throwing his rucksack on to the mattress.

They stood for a moment smiling at each other. Stefan was not much taller than Murielle, although he felt like a giant beside her. Then he remembered that he had something to give her, gesturing for her to wait while he rescued her page of drawings placed between leaves of his book for safe keeping. Murielle studied the drawings as if remembering each detail.

Stefan suggested they went for a drink, tipping his thumb towards his mouth and his head back, 'Beer? Bière? Cerveza?' she nodded, enthusiastically. They carried their boots, stopping at the door to replace them before they stepped out into the evening with the gentle air fresh on their faces. Stefan did not even mind that his feet hurt; he felt pleased with life and with Murielle especially.

There were other pilgrims sitting outside the bar; their faces glowed under streetlights. Stefan wanted Murielle to himself and fortunately there was a table a little away from the rest. They could not converse. There silences were punctuated with smiles and mime. Stefan explained that he made films, showing Murielle by dumb show and letting her look at the world through his meter. Her attempts to explain she was a sculptress, as she waved curvy outlines of women in the air and mimed hammering a chisel left them both helpless with laughter.

That night in the dormitory sleep belonged to others who guarded it with such an earthquake of snores that the urine in Stefan's bladder vibrated. He looked across at Murielle, who, although dead to the world, had the grace not to be snoring. When at last he reclaimed some sleep for himself, the snorers' loud clear up operations with industrial strength plastic bags snatched it back. He dressed quietly and quickly and still Murielle did not wake up. It occurred to him that if he left a note with his destination for that day it might at least convey a wish to meet up again. As he bent near her to tuck the folded paper into one of her boots the pallor and smoothness of her face, like an ancient, china mask, surprised him.

TEN

It was past midday and the sun was at its hottest when Dominic and Rosemary arrived in Santo Domingo. The town was preparing for its *comida*, the daily ritual of a decent meal and following *siesta* and everywhere was shut.

It had been another day with scant shade; another day walked hand in hand, fast and hard, but Dominic had been less chatty. He often repeated that he was tired. Sweat poured from his face and he let it drip as if the effort of mopping it was too great.

'I like walking with you,' he said and put her fingers to his lips and kissed them.

The refuge was housed in a convent. They entered a covered courtyard, dark and cobbled with wood that smelt of must and cedar. The relief of the shade was immediate. Two tiny Indian nuns in white robes took their details and showed them across the courtyard and up endless stairs like a maze. The rooms that opened off the corridor were small and cell-like. The diminutive white figure bid Dominic enter into one bedroom with a shove that nearly sent him sprawling and Rosemary was led down a corridor that wound away out of perspective, like a lithograph by Escher.

It was busy, everyone milling to and fro, unpacking rucksacks and heading for showers. Some faces were familiar; most were strangers. The bed/bathroom ratio was enough to raise a sigh.

The bedroom Rosemary was allocated had only four beds, two taken by a Spanish couple who looked like father and daughter. The girl was about fifteen, slight, dark and exquisitely pretty. The father fussed around her. He was encouraging her to finish Paulo

Coelho's book about the Camino that she was reluctant to read.

'*Pero bueno, Papa*,' a remonstration she murmured with a hint of sullen rebellion.

A striking looking young woman entered and slumped on the fourth bed without greeting anyone. Her hair was coiled in a towel adding several inches to her considerable height. She rummaged in her bag and withdrew a mobile phone. After several attempts to send a message she threw it on the bed and cursed, the vehemence of the one word had all the hallmarks. Then, Papa was edging sideways out of the bedroom at an alarming rate positively dragging his treasure with him. '*Pero bueno, Papa*.' His face, turned away from the tall girl towards Rosemary, was crimson. It was not the possible swearing that accounted for his discomfort. The tall girl was naked, but for her thongs; one pair partly covered her nether region and another pair of toe thongs protected the soles of her brightly painted feet. She made no attempt to cover herself or spare the poor man's blushes. Rosemary looked at the girl in all her plump, young loveliness and felt like slapping her.

Chairs were strewn in the convent garden amid overblown roses and wafting grasses. Set a little to one side was a tiled floor, lying amid the ruins of the garden like a Roman mosaic. In the middle of it there was an old wooden bench, most likely from a church. Rosemary lay on it on her stomach and tried to write her diary, a daily ritual, but there were too many distractions even in the siesta. Bees buzzed and she could hear Dominic speaking to a fellow Dutch woman. The Dutch fitted his mouth and sounded almost lyrical after his accented English, making a hushing sound like wind through leaves on a tree.

Enjoying the sun amid strings of washing, most of the men had taken off their shirts. One of the sisters marched purposefully through the garden, dipped gracefully under dripping shirts, socks and underpants, then stopped abruptly. Seeing the men with bare torsos she insisted that they put on their shirts. The men, young and old alike apologised and looked ashamed of their nakedness as they complied. The sister passed near Rosemary, and was on the verge of saying something, but changed her mind, slipping quietly away, head bowed, hands folded under the wide sleeves of her white robe. If she had insisted that Rosemary sat up, she would have obeyed.

Stefan appeared in the garden, with his rucksack still chinking. He looked hot and flustered as if he found it hard to settle in the relaxed atmosphere. Dominic introduced him to his companion, Ria, who was as brown as a suitcase and whose hair was cropped close to her head. They swapped from speaking Dutch to English.

'Please, not for me,' Stefan said.

'It is rude to exclude you,' she said

'I promise I won't get a complex.'

Ria laughed for a long time at that as if the word meant something different in Dutch. Then she excused herself, getting easily to her feet as if she had not just walked twenty miles that day. 'Nice to meet you,' and she was gone.

Dominic and Stefan sat forward in their chairs smoking cigarettes.

'I suppose you got a taxi,' Dominic said.

'No I walked,' Stefan bristled, 'It was not so far today having trudged all that way yesterday. What happened to you? You didn't turn up.'

Dominic waved his cigarette at nothing in particular, 'Oh you know.'

'No, I don't know and, on second thoughts, I don't want to.'

Dominic nudged him teasingly and clapped an arm round his shoulder.

'It's time to find a beer before we eat. Coming?'

'What about your conquest?' Stefan's voice was still angry.

Dominic rested his elbows on his knees. Smoke from his cigarette cast a veil over his face and he looked at Stefan through it, blowing out audibly. Stefan relented and mumbled, 'Ought to stow my stuff first, find a bed, take a shower. You better wait for me or I might never see you again.'

Dominic smiled, dimples creasing his face.

'It's a small place. You'll find me.'

'I'll come now, it will be easier.'

They walked side by side, like father and son; Dominic head and shoulders taller than his stockier companion. They were silent, but their shadows, stretched behind them, appeared to bend together as if deep in conversation.

Rosemary sauntered into town, clean, rested and feeling exposed without the heavy bag that she felt identified her as a pilgrim. It acted as a free pass, giving dispensation from the rigors of everyday life.

It was good to be alone and wander at will; this small town was very appealing. Not only did Santo Domingo have a cathedral and several other beautiful churches it even had a *parador;* a noblemen's palace, built right in the main square, now converted to a swish hotel. A glimpse of the courtyard was enticing. The light was diffused, there were patches of sun, patches of shade and tubs of flowers; the paving was decorous, the whole area clean and sweet smelling. She would have liked to let herself be drawn in, a place to sit from the glare of the world and just be for a while—a private place; an inner sanctum where even looking felt intrusive.

She was distracted by the sight of two horses tethered in deep shade by one of the buildings; piebald, with only a rope round their muzzles. She remembered her mother exclaiming at the cruelty whenever she saw horses in a field left with the bit between their teeth. They stood so still they could have been painted on to the wall except for the occasional twitch of an ear. She wished she had a carrot or an apple to reward the patient beasts. She made her way to them, speaking softly in English. One bent back an ear, but otherwise they took no notice. A man she had not seen appeared out of the gloom and stood protectively at the horses' heads and she asked him if he would sit on his horse so she could take his picture. These were the first horses she had seen on the pilgrimage. The man explained that he and his friend had walked from Bilbao, only occasionally riding their horses. She was impressed.

'It is a beautiful thing to walk with a horse,' and he gave her a leg up so she could appreciate it for herself. The horse's back was warm and the hairs smooth on her bare legs. Briefly she glimpsed the beautiful thing: the simplicity of faith and of man at one with nature. The horses soon drew a crowd and she felt foolish.

They stood patiently as pilgrim after pilgrim petted them; alternately patting noses, necks and flanks. The man returned to lean in the shade, one foot tucked up behind him against the wall.

'What is the matter with people? It's a wonder the

69

horses don't kick them. Haven't they seen a horse before?'

Stefan was tetchy and prepared to pass by, but Dominic pointed out Rosemary mounted on one of the horses' backs.

'I'm going to take a picture,'

Dominic pushed his way to the front to get a better shot.

'Thought she'd have more sense,' Stefan could not lift his mood.

'You must admit, Stefan, it's a classic.'

'It's tacky.'

'Here of all places.'

'It's still tacky. It's a show, *The Camino Show*. Why is the simple experience never enough for people? They always want more.'

'You've walked the Camino too many times, Stefan.'

Stefan threw down his cigarette and ground it with his boot. He felt cheated. All the effort he had put into his walk the day before in order to spend time with Dominic had come to nothing. He wasn't willing to admit that it was Dominic who had cheated him so he blamed the Camino, venting his anger on the institution and the poor simple souls walking. Even Rosemary was joining in—or being taken in. He turned on Dominic.

'The Camino panders to the worst kind of people, don't you think? Those who want 'different' or 'alternative' and, since the Camino is the place for miracles, there are those willing to make that happen. These aren't part timers with vestiges of some life of their own; these are the fully converted, signed up members addicted to the daily fix—dependent too for their livelihood, in some cases.'

Stefan did not want answers; he wanted to rant.

70

A little trace of spittle had worked its way to his upper lip. Dominic did not point it out and tried not to fix his gaze on it as the tirade continued.

'The Camino Show is born; a slow gestation evolved over centuries and continually re-inventing itself. It's not always easy to steer clear of this undercurrent tugging at the mainstream, powerful enough to sweep pilgrims and locals *á veau l'eau,* down stream, head over head, until neither party is certain who's creating the myths and miracles and who has the greatest need to believe in them. Both sides willingly suspend their better judgement and the alternative commerce, an over the top underworld, becomes believable.'

'Well,'

Dominic did not know what to say, but would acknowledge that neither the Camino nor Stefan's 'show' were for the fainthearted. He thought Stefan's view a little jaundiced; coloured perhaps by the stunt he had pulled the day before, sending Stefan to a different hostel. This was his punishment. He let Stefan have his say without further interruption.

'The comfiest garage, complete with a sing-a-long and a bake out, little more than a shack, a flimsy balsa wood construction with faith healer to keep off rain; an authentic ruined cathedral offering a nightly *queimada,* a ritual burning, for the delectation of all concerned; a tent, a yurt; you name it, they'll get it.'

Dominic retrieved a cigarette he had already rolled and tried his best to ignore the grumbling. He was impressed by the diatribe, by the young man's vehemence and surprised by his own meekness. He had loved the Camino even before he had set foot on it. He loved the legends, the history and the spiritual and arcane, even the profane. Run by entrepreneurs it catered for dreamers, both sides lost in their own propaganda and providing and using the sort of tacky in-house entertainment that the Church has majored in since; well he was not too well versed on church history, but at least since the days of hermits and the fortuitous appearance of the headless Santiago, warrior saint, returned to rid Spain of the Moors; Santiago Matamorros. That was Dominic's all time favourite legend; he had a picture of the saint riding out to battle in his office at home. Some days he found himself staring at the picture, the glorious folds of the blue cloak and especially the look in the eyes. He imagined the artist; he imagined the model and wondered what exactly had been said to promote that look. He had even tried to copy it, standing in front of a mirror and lifting his chin. That look came from within: some inner glow, some deep-rooted belief that he never did manage to capture. He had planned his itinerary so that he would stay at all the towns or villages where some legend had been born, some miracle had taken place, but so far he had not found what he was looking for.

If anyone was looking for miracles, or was in need of them—were such things to exist—it would be Stefan. This place, named after Dominic's own Saint, had invented a miracle. It had helped the town prosper in medieval times; it was still prospering. Dominic approved of the luxury of the *parador* and the other stately palaces that surrounded the square. The opulence of the cathedral fascinated him and as for the legend: who knows? Maybe the saint himself did intervene here. A young man praying to St James to save him from the gallows for besmirching the reputation of a nobleman's daughter was a conceivable concept for Dominic. He had been in similar scrapes as a young man, although not to the extent of being hanged or needing a miracle to save

72

him. If the townspeople were superstitious enough to believe the auspicious crowing of a cockerel was a sign from the almighty, or from St James, then that too was fine in Dominic's book. It was the cockerel he felt sorry for: a live cockerel shut in a gilded cage in the depths of the cathedral till the end of its days having to crow for its life.

Stefan had not finished.

'Typical Camino logic. If there isn't a miracle, invent one. And if one particular legend does not suit you, why not embroider it?'

In Stefan's version a German pilgrim was wrongfully accused of theft and it was the local dignitary's chicken dinner getting up and flying away when the young man's parents applied to him for justice that provided the divine intervention that saved the pilgrim.

'Dominic, you're obsessed with sex.'

'Oh, I don't think so, Stefan; a healthy interest maybe.'

If there was one thing Stefan understood, it was obsession. He could recognise the signs, the air of distraction, the light in the eyes fuelled by an inner fire. Obsession was perhaps too strong a word for Dominic. He was not yet so addicted that every waking moment was taken up, his mind running double speed so it could appear to be present in the here and now, but in fact was scheming, plotting, engineering events to satisfy the need. Perhaps the world turned on obsession and that was synonymous with, and is what fuelled, dreams. What did he know?

'Let's go to the cathedral, I want to hear the cock.'

Stefan was overjoyed when he heard the poor imprisoned cock crow. It was said to be a good sign for a pilgrim, the sign of a good Camino; and that was important for him.

ELEVEN

It was a balmy evening and, rather than incur the displeasure of the nuns by relaxing in the convent garden, pilgrims strayed to the square. Their murmured conversations wafted over the mellow stones as shade gradually encroached. Rosemary sat with Ria, enjoying a beer and listening as Ria talked philosophically in halting English. As she spoke she ran her fingers through her stubble short hair over the ridges and troughs of her skull as if to reassure herself of its solidity. Small round patches of alopecia, where downy traces of hair were growing back, would have been hardly noticeable had Ria's fingers not frequently sought them out.

Ria had been walking for two months already and had walked through France and thought she would take another month maybe to get to Santiago. One of those pilgrims who step out of their front door and start walking along any of the paths through Europe running to Santiago like water spilling out over the vast plane first in a trickle then a flood. She wasn't sure whether to go on to the coast, to Finisterra, another hundred kilometres or so after Santiago. She would see how the land lay when the time came.

'You say this also, I think. Maybe I will have enough already.'

Rosemary was impressed that anyone should undertake such an odyssey. She wanted to ask the pilgrim question, *Why are you walking?* but she hesitated, intimidated perhaps by this redoubtable woman or, sensing the chink in the confident exterior, afraid the story might be too personal. Instead she asked Ria what she did for a living and the answer to her underlying question came too.

'I am a paediatrician.'

It would not be hard to imagine children liking the kind eyes behind the horn rimmed specs that appeared overly large at some angles or taking hold of the competent hands now settled in Ria's lap with their fine long fingers, holding themselves still.

'And I'm a workaholic. I needed to rebalance my life. So I set off walking for three months.'

Rosemary felt a familiar stab of envy for any woman with a satisfying career. It had not happened for her; perhaps as having children just does not happen for some women; not necessarily a conscious decision. She hoped that Ria would not ask her what she did. She thought of all the jobs she had done: orthodontist's assistant, magician's assistant, shop assistant; something of a pattern. Had they not been temporary jobs she would have tired of them after a few months and longed for something new. Even after she had qualified as a teacher she had hated the commitment and resorted to supply teaching, which decimated the pay and any career prospects, but made the commitment bearable. She assumed that a professional woman, a self confessed workaholic, would despise anyone with this attitude to work, which she had once heard described in the dole queue as a waste of space. It became one of those fears that visited on sleepless nights.

She was curious to know how finances would be managed over three months with no work. Ria explained the principle and, either she thought Rosemary needed one-syllable explanations or the explanation really was simple.

'A year's sabbatical is an option for most workers: you take nine tenths of your salary for ten years and the final year you didn't have to work.'

'You've planned this walk for ten years?'

Ria laughed, her whole face puckered, and she took some time to straighten it. 'Not quite, but I have known for a long time that I would do it.'

'Yes, I suppose I knew that too.'

Nine tenths of Rosemary's salary over the last ten years would not amount to much even had the system been in place in England. Her trip was funded by an overdraft to be worried about on her return; not planned for ten years in advance. Forward planning was for tidy minds mapped out like a town with rows of straight avenues and a view ten years into the future. Her mind was more of an English country lane with all the bends and sidetracks. Rosemary need not have worried: Ria was not curious about her and neither asked what she did nor why she had come. Up to a point this was a relief; Rosemary was not sure she could formulate a coherent answer. It confirmed her suspicion that Ria assumed she had nothing interesting to say.

'I thought I needed a new life,' Ria continued, 'but after all the walking I know that it is not a new direction I need just a new attitude. What I have is fine; I like my life and I love my job. I just need some more breathing space. I get too involved and too tired, that's all.'

'Didn't someone famous say that? About looking at life with new eyes?'

'It's the basis of many religions and help groups.'

Rosemary was sceptical, but tried to maintain a look of benign interest. She thought Ria was misguided; no amount of good intentions ever changed attitudes; not for her, she always found herself back in the same situation sooner or later. Perhaps the secret was to keep trying. She wondered if only she could get involved in something, find a passion, she might feel better.

*

Stefan and Dominic ambled up and Stefan shuffled his feet while Dominic kissed Rosemary affectionately. It was his usual way of greeting her; an intimacy he did not extend to Ria. Dominic made a point of sitting beside her, reorganising chairs so that he could fit. Rosemary tried to avoid looking Ria in the eye, not wanting to see the knowing look, a mixture of superiority and disapprobation she was sure would be there. She was fond of Dominic: it was not a crime. Why should she feel that it was? It was simply a new situation that left her tongue tied like a teenager.

They were hungry and a waiter was summoned. Mostly the choice was fried eggs, which, for Rosemary, was the worst thing in the world. There was no ceremony to the meal and no substance either. Rosemary offered Dominic her eggs rather than waste them and he did not seem to mind eating four fried eggs. They disappeared rapidly and she thought he ate with the speed of one who comes from a large family. All of Seb's family ate so quickly it was impossible to say what their table manners were like as the food was finished before there was chance to look, except for Seb. When they had first met he ate extraordinarily slowly with a protective arm around his plate. She had laughed at the image of his brothers pinching food from him.

A group of pilgrims made their way noisily over the stone flags of the square with their shadows stretching behind them. One of them was the tall, sexy girl from her bedroom, so lovely that it hurt her eyes to look.

'Hey. It's the Flying Dutchman.'

Her accent was thick, Swedish maybe, and she looked Nordic; long, lean limbs, long, blonde hair almost white like ice and an attitude long on possibilities as if the world was rightly hers. She did not bother gazing at anyone else. George Clooney himself could have been in this sun-divided square and she would not have noticed. She sat on Dominic's knee and ran her fingers through his blonde halo of curls; Prince Charming remained impassive. So impassive that the girl got up after leaving a lingering slaver on his slightly bristly cheek, 'Fine, whatever, see you then.' She turned to her companion, an equally tall, loose limbed youth and muttered something in another tongue which sounded a little like, 'Motherfucker.' They strolled to where the shade drew a strict line and teetered momentarily on the edge to chat before disappearing with another young pair.

Rosemary had turned her head away deliberately not wanting to see the plump loveliness wrap itself round Dominic; march up boldly and take back one of his kisses. Really she had not seen them; she thought of a tortoise neatly tucking its head into its carapace. Ria looked at her pityingly and Rosemary feigned indifference.

'I hate that,' she heard Dominic say.

She was not surprised that a girl from a previous night was reclaiming his attention, but she did not comment. *What is it that you don't like Dominic, someone to play you at your own game? You shouldn't lead them on.*

Instead, she had smiled with a dismissive shrug, a gracious action and she had given him her fried eggs, a more subtle seduction. She looked across at the *parador* that was already in shade except for one door that was open and letting out sunshine and wanted to be in that garden. It must be physics or an architect's trick with the light, something Magritte would think of: to let sunshine out of a building.

TWELVE

Stefan could barely hide his anger.

'You're an animal, Dominic.'

'Sexy beast?'

'You just don't get it. You are old enough to be her father.'

'It's you who's not getting it. Jealous, maybe?'

'Disgusted, actually.'

Dominic shrugged his shoulders. Dimples creased his face. He did not understand Stefan. Women found him irresistible, so what? That was just as it had always been. He adored women, especially when they smiled at him. So why should it not be reciprocal? In fact it did matter, but he did not want to acknowledge how much. He hated the fact that aging mattered. He, Dominic Vandermeer, debonair lady killer, father of three, pillar of his community, playwright extraordinaire, was growing old; short of breath in the mornings, a little paunchy, the makings of jowls. At least his hair was not grey. And it mattered that women still found him attractive.

'You sound like an old man, Stefan.'

And for a moment it appeared the argument might escalate and neither wanted that.

'Come on, I'll buy you a drink. A beer is called for; San Miguel, maybe?'

'San Miguel it is.'

Their shadows stretched before them as they crossed the square, languorous slow-moving alter egos, relaxed in each other's company. In the shadow world nothing mattered, not difference in age or stature, not even differences of opinion. In two dimensions they had no importance; only in the flesh did it cause problems.

*

In the cool of the bar Stefan rationalised his anger. He was not prurient, but he believed in a strict moral code. He almost believed in God. Rather, he wished he believed in God. He did believe in romance and chivalry, Love with a capital L. He was disappointed that Dominic was so casual about it; not for love's sake, but because he wanted to hero-worship Dominic. If Dominic had feet of clay then perhaps his judgement on other matters was faulty. Perhaps *he* was wrong about love.

He certainly did not have much success with women. Nobody fell at his feet or batted their eyelashes at him, unless he could count Murielle. His spirits lifted briefly. No, he only wanted one woman. He unclenched his fists, rubbed his fingers gingerly over the scabs on his knuckles and took a long slow swig from his bottle of San Miguel. Blood began to pound in his ears as he remembered hammering on the door of her flat; his head hurting from the arguments of previous nights stretching back in a dizzying tailspin and the familiar sickness filled his belly. He loved her; he worshipped her. 'Why isn't that enough?' he remembered shouting, he knew he'd been sobbing. The memory of it drained him.

'So what's her name then? This girl who has your heart?' Dominic asked.

'Natalia, she's a Russian émigré.'

Dominic took a long swig of his beer, enjoying the cut of the cold bubbles at the back of his throat, and sighed.

'She's called Inge and I've known her since university. Love at first sight, but only on my part.'

'Not easy then.'

'We lived together for a while but things fell apart.'

80

Nothing in Dominic's life fell apart. Things were either fixable, in which case you fixed them, or broken and thrown away. But he knew that life was not so simple for everyone.

'And she has moved on, right?'

Stefan hunched over his beer; Dominic wondered if he wanted sympathy.

'I suppose you know the one about plenty of fish in the sea?'

Stefan scoffed. He knew the voracity of his unrequited love. It had the appetite of a wild beast that has scented blood. It chewed his heart every time he thought of Inge and he thought of her every minute of every day.

'And your film, is that about unrequited love?'

'No, it's a feel good film, a love story. There's enough kitchen sink stuff. If things can't come right in fiction what hope is there?'

Stefan tried to laugh, man of the world, who knows that life imitates art and, at times, becomes its pale reflection.

'The hero gets the girl of his dreams.'

Nice but dull, would have been Dominic's summation of the film.

'She isn't a cold hearted bastard who calls the police to put a restraining order,' Stefan's voice hardened as his throat constricted.

Dominic put a hand on his arm, as much to steady himself as to prevent Stefan from bursting into tears. He felt a wave of sympathy followed swiftly by a hot surge of anger. This was not a love he knew. He glanced at the abrasions on Stefan's hands and thought of stalkers and murder and looked questioningly at Stefan.

'I suppose you walked into a door?'

'I send her flowers every day and the last few

times I've been taking them myself. She didn't like my flowers.' Stefan spread his fingers; fine, manicured, artists' hands.

'Don't tell me you hit her?'

'Ok, I won't.'

Dominic was unsure where to go from here. He sipped his beer and wiped his mouth with the back of his hand.

'First, she slammed the door in my face and I heard her burst into tears. Next time she didn't answer the door and I shouted abuse at her till the neighbours told me to go away. The last time she took the flowers off me on the doorstep and swiped me about the head with them before throwing them at me and then she slammed the door. I punched the door, the wall, God knows what else I punched and, that time, I was the one in tears. The police took me away.'

Dominic could not speak for a while and he was glad Stefan continued to examine his hands and did not look at him.

'What are you going to do?'

'I've entered it in the Berlin Film Festival, but it will fail, I know it.' Stefan did not look up.

'No, Inge.'

'I'm going to forget about her.' Stefan put on a brave face.

'How long have you known her?'

'It will be our tenth anniversary when I get back from Spain.'

Dominic whistled. What kind of madness was this?

'I've promised myself that with every day's walk, every night under the stars, I will let go of her, little by little, till finally there will be nothing left.'

Dominic took time to reflect before replying.

'Want another beer?'

Stefan smiled. He had a flop of hair that gave him a boyish look. His smile was bright and Dominic noticed how perfect his teeth were.

'I'm not really mad.'

Dominic wasn't so sure.

'Tell me about your film.'

By the time they crossed the square, rejoining the clutch of chatting pilgrims, they were almost best of friends again. Two blokes, the bond they felt for each other firmly restored and Dominic, on surer ground, was asking Stefan's advice.

'The play I wrote,' Dominic started, 'the one that's starting a run when I finish the Camino; I wondered if you'd read it. I was thinking of adapting it as a screenplay and I'd like to know what you think. I'll email it to you.'

'I don't have an email address at the moment. I don't even have an address. I invested everything in making the film. When I go back I will start again with nothing.'

This information so upset Dominic that he could not speak. He thought Stefan truly was the last of the troubadours. He had risked all for a misguided ideal, not for love, but for a film that no doubt would fail. He tried again,

'Not even your parents?'

'I grew up in an orphanage.'

The square, now almost in darkness, had a party atmosphere. A hum of voices echoed off the buildings amid the sound of shutters being bolted up for the night. Other pilgrims lingered, even though café proprietors were putting away empty tables and chairs for the night. Dominic felt he needed some time under the stars, but not in rowdy company. He left Stefan in the square and sauntered slowly back to the convent.

He thought of Janneka and of what they had together; she was a wonderful woman. He usually only thought this way after too much beer, but he hadn't had nearly enough beer to digest what Stefan had told him. He thanked the stars for Janneka, for his parents, for being normal and able to cope with life. He didn't mean to be quite so smug. He felt utterly responsible for Stefan. How could an intelligent young man be in such a mess? Perhaps Stefan should come and stay with him for a while in his lovely Dutch countryside. Would his daughter be safe? A father has to think of these things. Yes, he thought, she would.

When he turned into the cobbled entrance to the convent courtyard there was no light other than stars and he leaned back into the shadows: a peaceful place. He lit a last cigarette, inhaling slowly. Rosemary entered the courtyard; she made him think of a little brown mouse.

'Hey!' He laughed when he saw her jump.

'God, you startled me.'

'Sorry,' he said, and when she came closer he pulled her into his arms and stooped to kiss her. He fumbled and missed her mouth.

She pulled herself away, 'You are so,' there was a pause and he waited to hear what she would call him; it was not what he expected. 'Tall.'

'Sorry,' he said, but could not explain why he felt the need to apologise.

In the bedroom with the doting father and the lovely daughter the night was quiet and still. Rosemary dreamt she was wandering in and out of the sunshine in the quiet of the courtyard that was also the untidy

84

convent garden with a golden patchwork of sweet smelling flowers. She watched unobserved as Dominic stooped to kiss a young girl whose hair was twisted in a towel on top of her head. They spoke a language she did not understand; a lilting of words with infinite numbers of syllables that echoed on her carapace, forcing her to withdraw.

By the morning she was convinced that she should say goodbye to Dominic and walk on alone. That is what she had come to do. Dominic had forced a fast, long pace. Although she was glad to walk thirty kilometres in a day, that distance was too much. She did not have the strength for that and thought it important to walk at her own pace.

She was hungry from not eating much tea the night before, but did not have provisions to make breakfast and hoped to find a bar open. Just before setting off she went to find Dominic who was awake, but not stirring.

'Dominic, I've come to say goodbye,' whispering to him and still managing to disturb his sleeping companions.

'So soon? You've had enough of me already' She was uncertain whether he was joking.

'Give me your email, yes?'

His fingers, still stiff with sleep, grasped the scrap of paper she held out where she had already written the address.

The portal in the huge wooden door that had allowed her to glimpse the courtyard the night before was firmly shut as she walked past, but the morning was fresh and still. The sun, fiery red, bestowed a pink tinge on everything it touched and the sky was eerily white by comparison. She thought it would be outrageously hot, but the white sky folded over the sun and the morning was cool. The quiet path

85

through fields gave way to a main road, which was tiring and noisy. It often appeared on these ancient paths that there was nothing between one village and another except wilderness, vast vistas diminishing to the horizon. It was a jolt to find a main road and the real world so close by. At least she knew that Burgos was forty-seven kilometres ahead and Logroño already sixty-four behind.

Solitude came during the day: hour after hour of tramping through desolate country sometimes not even a distant village to remind her that it was still the same century. Occasionally, after hours alone, she stumbled into a village and there would be a pile of rucksacks heaped outside a café and pilgrims comfortably having their elevenses. It would be all she could do to stop herself saying, 'Oh, there you all are.' People who had been still in bed when she left, those she had never seen before, all mysteriously got there before her. Occasionally cyclists hurtled up behind, ringing their bells, shedding ugly chocolate wrappers and kicking up the dust snapping her back to the present.

Have I told you lately that I love you?

The words of Van Morrison's song, more of a prayer, that Seb sometimes sang to her filled her head. He surprised her with romantic gestures; he was not a sentimental man. Lately when she heard it, or even thought of it, the words rather jumbled themselves in her head so that it was the gladness taken away and the heart that filled with sadness. She tried to think of another song, something positive: *She who would valiant be,* perhaps.

THIRTEEN

There had been no sign of approaching a town, no mounds of rubble or barking dogs snatching at heels to bring her back to earth. One moment she had been day dreaming the next she was on the outskirts with a refuge beside the path.

'Eldorado, the Most Romantic Garage,' read a sign painted rather inexpertly above the open door. The spreading branches of old fruit trees cast shade over a few white plastic tables and chairs set out neatly in front of the garage for the benefit of pilgrims. She flopped gratefully pressing her eyelids closed till the misery of her blisters gradually subsided.

A woman bustled between tables placing baskets of plums and pitchers of water that tinkled with ice, 'Help yourselves,' she said in English, and Rosemary looked round to see who else was there. José Luis was camouflaged in dappled shade and she could almost hear the scrape of his pen over the photocopied page of his guidebook. He did not look up. She unlaced her boots, eased her feet out and gingerly peeled off her socks. She expected blood and gore considering the amount of pain there had been and her feet were in a sorry state. She unpacked her sensible sandals, placing them on the ground beside her. Had she heeded any advice to practise walking with a laden rucksack before setting off, she might have discovered that carrying the extra weight would make her feet spread so that her once comfortable boots became too small.

As she was ramming the boots into her rucksack the woman called out to her, 'You cannot possibly expect to walk hundreds of kilometres through the mountains in sandals. You will go lame.'

All self-pity evaporated.

'Oh?'

That short English phrase whose different intonation can cover all eventualities. Rosemary hoped that she stopped short of brusque and rude, but she doubted it. She had compressed a gamut of feeling into the one word, 'what's it to you, mind your own business, fuck off,' and felt mildly ashamed at her out burst. Rosemary took out her notebook and chewed a pencil nonchalantly. Jose Luis summoned the woman with a silent gesture almost as if he was holding court and she was his slave and must do his bidding. The woman disappeared into the romantic garage reappearing a few moments later carrying a large bowl. This she placed on the ground in front of Rosemary and then lifted Rosemary's feet into it with a gentleness that belied her gruff tone. The water was warm and smelled gently of disinfectant and the relief was instant.

'You really must take care of yourself.' She smiled in such a motherly way that Rosemary had to concentrate hard not to give in to tears.

The Flying Dutchman came into view, swinging round the corner of the romantic garage, full of rude vigour. He stopped to take a plum, tossed it a couple of times in his palm before stooping to plant a kiss on Rosemary's upturned lips. The kiss was snatched and not gentle.

He tried to persuade her to walk the next ten kilometres to a quieter hostel. He would be staying there and he was sure she would like it.

She was non-committal, even if her heart did miss a beat.

When she glanced in José Luis' direction, wondering what he would make of the kiss and why she should want his good opinion, he was collecting his things together as if he had not witnessed it. He walked towards her so self assured and handsome and asked if there was anything he could do to be of assistance. His manner was centuries old, a whole tradition passed down through generations, perhaps from the time of Knights Templar protecting maidens from rogues along the Camino or rescuing them from Moorish infidels who stayed over six hundred years in Spain. When she smiled and said she was fine he produced a large packet of sweets with a slight incline of his head. '*Caramelos, Rosa Maria.*' When she declined the offer he insisted that she take a handful. Then in nearly unrecognisable English, with words mangled almost beyond repair, he said, 'Remember Churchill, Rosa Maria. You must never give up.'

She had no intention of giving up, but collapsed in a heap, must have looked to Jose Luis and to the woman *hospitalero* as if she would not make it.

The one room of the romantic garage was fully bunked and several of the early morning rustlers, whose inexplicably loud plastic bags destroy sleep anytime after five in the morning, were already tuning up. She pictured them in a semi-circle, a small balding conductor with expressive eyebrows, playing the first performance of a specially commissioned piece; smiling on their once slumbering audience on whom they practiced their art: the ancient art of sleep deprivation using modern plastic techniques. She decided to delay her decision to stay or move on and at least look at the town first.

For most inhabitants of any town along the Camino, the stream of pilgrims adds little to the general tide.

Citizens go about their daily life. Bank tellers run to the local butchers and queue for meat for the midday meal; children fall off bicycles; toddlers are pushed on swings and babies are rocked in prams by fragile *abuelas;* old men tend kitchen gardens and saunter home with armfuls of greens; teenagers stop to text friends from street corners as pilgrims sail by. Sun blasted, wind-blown, footsore, lean, fit and bronzed, young, old and in between, pilgrims of every hue, race and creed often leave no trace of their passing, their humpback outline no more than an impression on the retina that those living along the Camino must have come to accept since early childhood and cease to notice.

For most pilgrims, it is enough to go with the flow; enough to observe and be a foreigner in a strange land; to pass open doors of restaurants and see cool dining rooms filled with workers in blue overalls sitting easy with their shirt sleeves still rolled, breaking bread with their colleagues and waiting to be served; enough to mouth a half remembered prayer and admire the architecture in the local church, be it humble twelfth century stone, lovingly carved by craftsmen yearning for a place in the hereafter or magnificent and gold encrusted from the school of long forgotten masters certain of their right to a place.

The square, which was more a pentagon, bustled. Great hoops of flowers arched over the heads of the crowd and troupes of young boys and girls stood expectantly in red silk shawls shot with brightly embroidered flowers. Even when they stood still the tassels hanging from the shawls shimmied. Black clad ladies fussed about them. It was a lovely sight and a privilege to see this glimpse of Spanish life.

A reed pipe started to play and the crowd fell

respectfully silent, then stood back to allow the children to take the stage. After the dancing, with much twirling and jumping and ducking under the flower hoops, families set about the business of eating. The dancers in shawls followed their unrelentingly smart relatives into peaceful dining rooms. Rosemary retreated to a bar where the long afternoon and the pleasure of the spectacle slowly dissipated. Initial excitement at finding internet access faded to disappointment when there were no messages from home.

Rosemary began to feel rested enough to contemplate moving on, lured by the prospect of a quiet hostel, a good night's sleep and Dominic's company. All day alone is peaceful, all evening in the company of strangers, rather sad. Ten kilometres can be walked in two hours if the pace is brisk, but she felt leaden. The path, however, was quite shaded, winding through hedgerows. Rounding one corner she came on Stefan and a young girl sitting together on the grass verge, sharing fruit and biscuits. The girl invited her to join them so pleasantly that she sat a while and ate some fruit as it was offered. The girl had hypnotic violet eyes and was charming. Stefan gave the impression that he wanted her all to himself. He was swearing and posturing as if to impress the girl and Rosemary was surprised how uncomfortable he seemed in their company. She did not stay long and waved goodbye without a backward glance in case she should interrupt some tender moment.

FOURTEEN

It was no time till the next village, as if the guidebook had the distances wrong or a kind soul had moved it nearer. *Tosantos,* All Saints, was an unassuming hamlet and the hostel was housed in a humble tumbledown house set in a peaceful corner surrounded by the ghost of a garden and a forest of plastic chairs. Dominic, in characteristic pose, legs stretched out in front of him, soaking up the last of the sun, appeared to own the place. He turned his head as Rosemary limped on. He smiled, but did not move.

'You look comfy,' she said.

Dominic turned his head back towards the sun.

The *hospitalero* came in to the garden carrying a bowl of water, 'I saw you limping,' he said.

'Is that for me?' Rosemary could not believe the kindness.

Dominic watched as she lowered her feet into it and turned away at the sight of blood leeching into the water. The *hospitalero,* clicked his tongue, 'Let me dress your feet.'

He brought a little box of sponges and bandages. He cut sponges to fit round the blisters to relieve the pressure and with infinite tenderness bound up Rosemary's feet.

'They will heal now,' he said and picked up the bowl of water to take it back inside the house.

'Come, I'll show you where you can sleep.'

She followed him along a flagged corridor and up wooden stairs. The house was cool and smelled of dust. They stopped at the door to a large room, empty except for one sleeping bag laid out on bare boards and Dominic's rucksack propped against the wall. He gestured for her to make her resting place next to it and stood beside her, supervising while she unpacked her sleeping bag.

She asked his name and he looked surprised.

'Call me Jaime.'

'I wanted to thank you Jaime for tending my feet.'

'Perhaps you can do something for me in return?' and seeing her look of dismay, however grateful she might be for the more comfortable feet, he added, 'Later, when you are rested. Why don't you enjoy the garden for a while?'

Dominic was turning an old cloth sewing kit over and over in his hands.

'This belonged to my father. My mother gave it to me when he died.'

He wanted her to see it. Tiny brass thimbles and cotton reels of every colour were still packed neatly as if both new and original owner had treasured it over the years. Rosemary was about to compliment him on how well it had been cared for when Stefan arrived with his young companion creating an energy surge in the tranquil garden. His rucksack, launched from a distance of several feet, thudded on a nearby chair. His voice seemed to boom and his companion's violet eyes distracted Dominic as his gaze followed her into the hostel. Stefan harrumphed and Dominic ignored him, turning back to Rosemary to ask if she would cut his hair. He handed her the scissors from his sewing kit. They had such small blades Rosemary knew it would be a disastrous cut.

'I don't have a comb,' she said.

'Does it matter?'

She stood behind Dominic, his head tipped back rested warm against her belly. She used her fingers to tease out the ends of his silver blond ringlets that were surprisingly soft. The scissors snipped away. Rosemary's fingers delved the mass of Dominic's curls again and again and wisps of hair floated on the gentle breeze with the clicking of the scissors and the soft rustling of leaves.

'He'll be bald if you keep that up.' Stefan's voice startled them.

'Aren't you worried she'll sap your strength?'

Dominic did not even turn his head and he did not answer. Perhaps it was a metaphor too far. Stefan stalked off into the refuge letting the door bang behind him.

'Oh dear,' Rosemary said, 'You do look a bit like a prisoner.'

Dominic laughed. 'It will grow.'

He looked at her expectantly as if he had done her a service and she should thank him for releasing some of her straight-laced, English inhibitions.

When it was time to prepare the evening meal of pasta and a sauce, Jaime fussed in and out of the kitchen. He took out vegetables from a store cupboard and asked Rosemary and Violet Eyes for help. At first he supervised, telling Rosemary to chop the vegetables more finely, but seeing that Violet Eyes, whose name was Judith, was very efficient he decided to leave them to it.

The kitchen was rather gloomy and felt oppressive. No sun came through the small, high window and hardly any light. Rosemary and Violet eyes spoke only an occasional word amid the sound of onion skins ripping away and the chop of knives against wooden boards, the drip of the tap. The quiet domesticity and the girl reminded Rosemary of home. She thought of her daughter whose birthday it was the following day: there would be no cake, no hugs, no fuss from her. The fact that the daughter in question had already left home and would anyway be having her cake and hugs and fuss elsewhere, was incidental. She thought of her birth: her eyes had opened as soon as she was born, large, bright eyes like lamps, already taking in the world, as if to see who she had won in the lottery of mothers.

A few quiet tears rolled down Rosemary's cheeks. She sniffed and blamed the onions, but her chopping got slower.

Then Stefan burst through the door and took charge. He rifled the store cupboard and chopped everything there was, including some bananas, and added all the herbs he could find. He tasted the sauce, repeatedly putting the spoon back in and complaining that the meal would be 'fucking tasteless' if they didn't watch out.

'Stefan,' Violet Eyes remonstrated.

'These *hospitaleros* make money out of pilgrims, you have to watch them.' Stefan would have gone on.

'Stefan!' Now it was Rosemary's turn. 'How can you say that? When everything is done out of the goodness of their hearts, free and for nothing?'

'Oh, they do.'

He would not be dissuaded till Dominic stuck his head round the kitchen door and beckoned him, leaving Rosemary and Violet eyes to stir the meal.

Dominic smelled onions and saw tears and knew the onions were not to blame. The domesticity of the scene reminded him of all that was wrong with society and he was walking to forget. He worked with disaffected youth of dysfunctional families and that was fine and he was good at his job. Now, though, he needed a beer. He wanted male company: rude, vigorous and earthy.

*

The bar was empty but for the two of them.

'Pilgrims keep this place going, I reckon,' Stefan said and ordered two beers, shaking his head when the bar tender offered him a glass. He looked over his shoulder at the television in one corner of the room. News of Iraq; but neither of them understood Spanish well enough to follow what was going on.

'Bloody Americans; two world wars not enough.'

Dominic turned to look at Stefan,

'I thought you said you had no luck with girls.'

'She is studying philosophy and our conversation has been deep and meaningful.'

'It's just a bonus that the child is so pretty.'

'Schopenhauer, Kierkegaard and Nietzsche; I am optimistic for Germany's future.'

Dominic stopped baiting Stefan.

'So, how was your walk today?'

'Good, I bumped into Judith of the violet eyes and managed to walk all the way without feeling my blisters. But, you're right, she's much too young.'

When they finished their beer they stared at the television where some woman in tears was standing outside the ruins of her home. Stefan looked at his watch and they got off their stools to saunter back.

'Give me that list of hostels, will you?' Stefan said as if he had suddenly remembered. Dominic put his cigarette in his mouth, squinting at the smoke getting in his eyes and reached for his wallet. He gave Stefan a folded sheet of paper.

'I'm not sure I can keep up your pace, but I wanted to be able to find you.'

Dominic smiled, trying to keep an expression of fatherly concern from his face. If Stefan thought meeting up every evening was helpful, then that was fine by him.

'D'you know Stefan, I think you should come and work with me back in Holland for a while. Assistant Artistic Director at the theatre—something along those lines.' He fished out his wallet again, took out his card and handed it to Stefan, 'Just so you know I'm serious.'

Stefan rubbed his forehead, an idiosyncrasy Dominic had noticed before.

'Thank you.'

There was an expression of such hopelessness in his eyes that Dominic blustered, clapping his back in a manly way as if to impart some of his energy.

'Must be nearly time to eat.'

He hoped he and Janneka had packed enough happy days under their children's belts to see them through hard times.

Half a dozen cyclists arrived late and noisily at the refuge, still fired by their speed, immediately sucking the peace and the tendency to melancholy out of the place. The lilting slowness of the walkers who, tired from their day, were noiselessly writing was replaced by braying laughter and ribald jokes. Jaime asked Rosemary to lay six more places at the table while he cut more bread and boiled extra pasta.

The cyclists, firemen from the south of Spain, had such energy it was impossible not to feel upbeat in their company.

'Ah, English!' One said, discovering Rosemary's nationality. A friend of his had gone to England to work and had got so depressed by the end of a year, what with the weather and the food and everyone else so miserable, that they had advised him to come back to Spain before it was too late. Ha Ha!

Jaime gave them the task of washing up after the meal and they agreed good-naturedly. He asked

Dominic to lay the table for breakfast, since he had not helped get the meal and Stefan laughed. 'Quite right, that's only fair.'

'Wasn't there something you wanted me to do?' Rosemary asked him.

'No, no, you have done enough.'

That night on the wooden floor of the dormitory that smelled of dust, with their sleeping bags side by side, Dominic extended an arm so Rosemary could lie in the crook of it. She curled up beside him, ready to fall asleep instantly. He whispered coaxingly in to her ear, 'Take what you want.'

Rosemary did not have the chance to say, 'I just want to lay my head on your chest and sleep soundly.'

She was asleep and neither the shaking of her shoulder, nor the slightly bemused, 'Hey,' repeated a couple of times, managed to rouse her sufficiently to take advantage of the magnanimous offer.

In the morning she set off alone. Dominic was still asleep and there was no sign of Stefan or his companion with the violet eyes. The cyclists were eating breakfast standing up, as if they really did not have the time. They raised their coffee cups to her in farewell. On her way out she noticed a donation box by the door with a notice saying, 'Pay what you can: take what you need.'

FIFTEEN

Stefan lounged in heather, cushioned and comfortable. The wind in his hair felt warm and pleasant after the closeness of the trees. He had worked up an appetite after the morning's walk, but had not stopped for fresh provisions. When he saw Rosemary he invited her to lunch, hoping that she would have what he needed. He put out his jars of olives and roast peppers and artichokes and she produced fresh bread and cheese.

'No chorizo?'

'This is best Manchego. Besides it's hard to keep chorizo from stinking out the bag.'

'I was joking.'

'Oh.'

She tore the bread apart and stuck a penknife in the wedge of cheese and he offered his olives.

Stefan did not want company or chat but he did want bread and, failing chorizo, cheese. He pulled the cork out of a half drunk bottle of red wine with his teeth and offered her the bottle, which he knew she would refuse.

She asked him about his young companion of the night before.

'She was a child, too young for me. Actually she was walking with a group of very earnest young people. Not my thing at all.' Stefan mentioned the sly old goat from the convent, the one with the very young girl friend, the one reading Paulo Coelho.

'Now *she* was stunning, the old goat'

'That was his daughter.'

'Are you sure?'

'Absolutely, we were in the same bedroom.'

'Fucking impossible.'

Rosemary accused him of having a polluted mind and a mouth full of swear words. The accusation made him blink; he was thoughtful for a moment and looked into Rosemary's green eyes to see if she was joking. She wasn't. He settled further into the heather with the bottle.

'You look like it's siesta time,' she was brusque, 'see you later, maybe.'

He didn't reply. He watched her struggle with her bag and rejoin the path. He watched till she got smaller and then he closed his eyes.

Dominic sat at a crossroads. He rested against the huge studded door of an ancient church. His long legs stretched in front of him and he had a splendid view from four different directions at once, without being seen himself. The village of Clavijo was perched high above the plain where Santiago Matamorros, headless and on horseback, lead the Christians to victory. Dominic tried to imagine how it might have been; clashing of weapons, heat, dust, cries of dying and wounded, the battle cry of the triumphant saint inspiring his men.

Wind whistled. That was one reason why he had his back to the door, to keep off the wind. He dozed in the afternoon sun but was not relaxed. He shook his head to deter a persistent fly, but his head was shorn and hot and he did not feel the reassuring bounce of curls. The fly persisted. He tried to think calm thoughts, but he was at a crossroads. Normally he would at least have smiled at the metaphor. Crossroads, come on. He chided himself.

He had done well, as always, to get this far so early in the day. He could move on: he had time, but the distance to the next stop was too far for Stefan who had not yet arrived and would probably attempt to follow him. If he stayed he would meet up with Rosemary and he wanted to spare both of them. She had proved she was not a conquest and he was ready to give up. Enough was enough. Or, he could stay and let her know this was her last chance. This was a place for victory, after all: Saint James the Moor slayer; Dominic the lady-killer: it did have a ring.

Then he saw her, a minute dot in the distance, plodding up the steep pilgrim path. How did he know it was her? She got under his skin and not necessarily in a good way. He sighed. He had told Janneka about her in his letters home, his long, chatty love letters.

She is small, her hair is grey and blond and her face is red in the sun and after any amount of red wine, however little. I like her but it doesn't stop me missing you. I like the way she can walk fast and nearly keep up with me. She makes me think of the robin that sits on our garden path when the sun shines and we are together.

I am ready for new company; except for the young man Stefan, the one I told you about. He will know where he can find me for the time that I am on the Camino. Maybe we should set an extra place for him at my homecoming. I would like to invite him to share our family meal. I think this must be missing from his life; a sense of family and belonging that you, dear Janneka, know how to provide.

I miss you more than I can say and I am finding this experience hard. Perhaps that is part of the joy; I think the walking and the separation are making me stronger and strengthening what we have between us. Give the children a hug from me.

Stefan trudged across the plain. The earth was parched and so was he. He could see his destination in the distance, not getting any closer. The village

101

Dominic had mentioned (at some length) was perched high above the plain on the edge of a precipice. Stefan tried not to think of the climb up to it. He wished he had not slept for so long, or drunk so much wine after lunch. He wished he had some company. He slipped his phone out of his pocket. There was not even a signal. He put the phone away and kept walking. He fingered his light meter and tried to focus on his film. He pictured the small auditorium as the lights dimmed, the moments of black before the swish of curtains and the screen sparking to life. His life, he thought, part of him exposed on the screen. For one bleak moment he thought of the personal cost. He had given everything. He pictured the audience, their few expectant coughs and rustles of sweet papers and tried to guess their emotions and those of the judges. What might they experience when they saw the huge heads, huge faces in close up and the camera panning out to show the whole opening scene? Now he was lost in the story and the emotions were no longer those of the audience, but his own. Some days he could sense the beauty of his film; others he could sense only triteness and failure. To have given everything and still fail was a bitter lesson.

Half a dozen buzzards circled above. Scavengers. He pictured them swooping to pick the bones of men and women slain in battle, horribly mutilated bodies, some not yet dead, too weak to fend the buzzards from taking their eyes.

He thought of Rosemary's comment that his head was full of vile images; he thought of Dominic's stories of Santiago, warrior saint riding into battle to save the Christians. He thought of the pilgrims who walked across the parched path and then he thought of the long cold beer he would have with Dominic.

Rosemary found the hostel nestled amid close-built stone houses in the village and dumped her bag on the first available bunk. In the room of about a dozen bunks, wooden shutters were pulled, blotting out the fierce sun and most of the light. A few pilgrims slumbered, recumbent figures like St Exupéry's drawing of the snake that has swallowed an elephant. She did not want to disturb them or stay in the gloom nor yet get straight in the shower.

José Luis emerged from the bathroom, clean-shaven and sweet smelling. He bowed and when Rosemary opened her mouth he said, '*Adios.*' It was labour saving; a cut-the-crap-but-lets-be-civil-about-it social nicety. He did not want small talk.

Rosemary went to explore and made her way to the cliff edge where the wind was stiff in her face. She stood looking out over a vast area of nothing. Somewhere, way below was the path for tomorrow that would lead to Burgos; impossible to imagine or locate, since there was nothing discernible in any direction. Huge birds cart wheeled above and appeared close enough to reach up and touch. Eagles, perhaps, with fronded wings on joy skimmed thermals. It was easy to believe great battles, even miracles, had taken place here.

An old woman had come up beside her, silent as the eagles in the vastness of the sky. She did not acknowledge Rosemary, but stood facing out to the emptiness as if any moment she would plunge off the cliff. There was no joy in her gaze.

'My daughter lives in Burgos; so far away,' she said.

A great wave of sadness carried the woman here to keep vigil. A distance of twenty miles separated the village from the city across the plain, a cavernous divide. The woman turned and went as silently and quickly as she had come. Rosemary did not turn to watch her go; it was just possible that sadness had washed her away.

Later, intent on writing her diary, out of the wind and the way of other pilgrims, Rosemary dozed; pen in hand, aware of the sun warming her body.

She opened her eyes when a shadow passed over the sun, waking with the surprise of one who does not know they have been sleeping. Stefan was leaning over her.

'Hello Stefan, take a load off and let the sun get to me.'

He squatted awkwardly,

'Hello.'

Rosemary closed her eyes, mildly irritated that he had woken her.

'I wondered if you'd like to play chess.'

She opened her eyes. 'Chess?'

And he shook a wooden box he had in his hand so that the pieces rattled.

'Chess; that *is* what you call it?'

She sat up pulling her shirt down where she had tucked it up to expose her flesh to the sun.

'I'm rubbish, I warn you.'

'That's ok,' and he cast about for a flat stone to rest the board on. The lid of the box opened out four fold, small hinges locked it into place and Stefan began to set the pieces starting with a row of pawns. This was not a common chess set. She picked up a piece to examine it.

'Do you often play?' she asked.

'It's a versatile game. You're never alone with a chess set.'

Rosemary wanted to laugh, but Stefan was so serious and she did not want to hurt his feelings.

As the game progressed her pieces disappeared rapidly into Stefan's hand.

'I did warn you.'

'I'm not playing to beat you, I'm playing to learn about the way you think.'

As a tactic in spoiling an opponent's concentration it was very effective. Rosemary felt uncomfortable, as if she was being asked to bare too much of herself and was unsure how to reply or whether to toss the board in the air, pieces and all, and say, 'analyse that.'

Sun reflected off the huge flat stone. Rosemary was comfortable with her back against a rocky outcrop but Stefan kept shifting his position, grinding his boots in gravel against stone. It was a relief when Dominic arrived, ambling up the steep incline. He kissed Rosemary and even Stefan assumed that the game was at an end.

'Anyone want a beer?'

'Why not?' Stefan and Rosemary answered together.

The bar was empty when they arrived and the bartender glanced reluctantly from the television screen that enthralled him. A musical in Technicolor, the colour so deep the characters could have come from Mars, not South Pacific. He served them lazily, taking time to pour three beers from a large bottle, his gaze constantly drawn back to the telly. Finally, just as Dominic was about to remonstrate, he slapped the beer in front of them with a smile, 'I've seen it before. It's always on.'

They were in good spirits when they arrived in the restaurant where a modest evening meal was provided for a modest sum. There was space at a table where two women were already seated.

Rosemary sat beside them; they were Danish but spoke English for Rosemary's benefit. Dominic and Stefan sat side by side, opposite, and ignored everyone. They were skittish; their game, if it was a game, sounded insulting, male banter mostly in German. Some of their comments and glances were directed straight at the Danish women and at Rosemary. She tried not to mind, pretending not to notice the rudeness, turning her attention to her Danish companions. They were comparing notes on unfaithful husbands.

'My husband has taken another.'

'Mine too. It's awful.'

She could see José Luis at another table and wished there had been room to sit with him. She left before the end of the meal and made her way back to the hostel, wanting to clear her head.

In the shower the phrase reverberated in the blissfully warm water, *He has taken another.* Rosemary practised it, attempting to authenticate the accent and to let the phrase dip with accusation and disgust as it had when spoken by the Danes. She realised that the women never actually said what their husbands had taken. It could have been anything from overdoses to motorbikes. She had assumed they meant lovers. *My husband has taken another. Mine too. It's awful.*

As she cleaned her teeth at the sink, she could see Dominic beside her bunk. He began shunting the bed with a loud grating noise, using his shins, till two bunks were together and the mattresses touched. He ignored everyone else in the dormitory and no one commented. She finished cleaning her teeth, examined them in the mirror with a grimace and passed Dominic on his way to the bathroom. As she could not get between the bunks, she moved them away a little before climbing into her sleeping bag.

Dominic shunted the bed back again to close the gap and got into his sleeping bag. They lay with their heads close enough to smell toothpaste on each other's breath. Dominic smiled and she eyed him.

'What was the matter with you and Stefan at dinner time?'

It appeared Dominic was not going to answer. He closed his eyes as if to blot out the question. Then he said, 'Those women were ugly and ate with their mouth's open so the food dropped back on to their plates. You should be careful too. You put too much in your mouth at once.'

'I am just glad I'm not a man.' Rosemary was annoyed.

She would have said, *you can go off people, you know.* Perhaps that is what Dominic meant in a roundabout way.

He was asleep immediately. She watched his lids droop and extinguish the startling blue of his eyes. When she turned over, Stefan's bunk had also made its way closer to hers; so close that to get up she would have to wriggle out at the bottom of the bunk. She fretted, tossing and turning, making all nine bunks shudder. She dreamed of motorbikes lined up outside her front door and Seb saying nonchalantly, 'I have taken another, you were away too long; it was awful.'

The early morning rustlers were on cue just as Rosemary had finally closed her eyes. Anger hissed from Stefan's sleeping bag, creating a force field, an impenetrable seething of sighs. He muttered threats to strangle everyone. Dominic slept on oblivious, still, completely encased in his sleeping bag. He was positioned diagonally so that he could fit the length of the bed, snoring gently and Stefan added him to the list of those to be strangled. Rosemary felt the need to intervene and put a steadying hand on top of Stefan's sleeping bag. She aimed for a neutral spot centre chest, patting and soothing as one would an angry toddler. At first she could feel him bridle; his chest was hard as armour. It gradually softened as his breath became more regular and he finally came off the boil.

SIXTEEN

A taxi dropped Stefan in Burgos in time for breakfast, a relaxed civilised affair, with a surprise twist. Murielle happened to be in the café he chose. He liked the hand of fate that brought them together and felt he needed something beautiful this morning.

'*Bien?*' he asked her.

'*Oui, tout est bien.*'

He didn't believe her. There was a light in Murielle's eyes that he could not place; an enticing mixture of fragility and strength, almost an ethereal, dreamlike quality. He read her newspaper over her shoulder and tried to decode headlines by looking at the photographs. She didn't seem to mind him sitting so close and he remembered not to chew in her ear. He wasn't really interested in what was happening in the world, at least not until he went home to Germany and then he would give the news his full attention. He suspected pilgrims were exempt from attending to world affairs. The church would surely give them dispensation. He had a vague idea of the plot to invade Iraq, but he already knew that the world was a mad, obsessive place. You would have to be obsessed or British to fight in a war; Germany was well out of it. He had a feeling of impotence when it came to politics. He was a small fry and nothing he said or did was of any consequence, unless, of course, by some miracle, his film was a success. Then perhaps it could be. He stopped reading and leaned back to take in the view. The thought of his film momentarily winded him, he felt a stab of lingering pain like a bitten tongue and he needed to think of something else. He watched Murielle as she ate, delicately dipping croissant into her coffee and then into her mouth. She reminded him of a gazelle and any moment she would take fright and dart away.

After this companionable breakfast and before the business of walking he intended to see part of the old Burgos. He stood up and invited Murielle to accompany him, making a little walking gesture with his fingers. She shook her head, but thanked him graciously. He would have liked her company all day, but somehow he knew she would not want to walk with him. Still, there was the prospect of a meander through the medieval streets and he was sure he would find specialist food shops with something delicious for lunch.

'*Adieu*,' and he bowed, just slightly.

'*A la prochaine fois,*' her smile was a delight and he sincerely hoped there would be a next time. He would have liked to tell her that he found her enigmatic, an appreciable quality.

Then Murielle changed her mind. 'Stefan.' He could not help smile hearing his name in her mellifluous voice. She took his arm and they sauntered and, for a whole hour, it was delightful. When Murielle wanted to sit again, Stefan was undecided; he wanted to stay, but he needed to walk. He touched his phone, he checked his light meter, he rubbed his forehead; he checked from under his fop of hair that Murielle had not seen him do these things. She pretended she hadn't.

'*Je suis telement fatiguée*, so *ti*-red,' and he knew she was letting him go.

It had been a trudge. Rosemary sat in the dust in wasteland, half way to nowhere, taking in the grim view. The path wrapped round mounds of moved earth, as if deliberately meandering a long way. There

110

were neither trees nor vegetation, as if an earthmover had flattened everything in sight and scooped out the red earth to form an enormous pit the size of an arena. Perhaps a film director had ordered the vast dust bowl in preparation for a scene of apocalypse.

Rosemary was hungry. There had been no bars serving steaming coffee or sticky buns. The gruff *hospitalero* had warned the pilgrims that there was no provision for breakfast, shrugging when one pilgrim had interjected, 'But, why didn't you say before, when we could have done something about it?'

She saw Dominic, making his way along the dirt track. He appeared alternately closer then further away; another filmic device.

He joined her in the dust, unsmiling.

'You ok?' she asked, 'You seem a bit, oh I don't know, down, perhaps.'

'Just tired.'

'Oh.'

'I am losing weight. And missing home.'

'Oh.'

'Are you?'

'Losing weight, missing home or tired?'

Dominic stood up and pulled Rosemary to her feet.

'Come on. It's a long slog in to Burgos, main road all the way. The thought of it is making me tired.'

He kept hold of her hand and she smiled at him,

'You don't have to follow the main road into Burgos, not according to my guide. Follow me.'

Then she said, 'And, I am losing weight and I do miss home, but not all the time.'

They were silent and concentrated on moving fast; the old rhythm that had felt so good. Rosemary felt foolishly glad; a chosen one with Dominic holding her hand; and wondered why it mattered so

111

much that he did like her after all. Heavy lorries thundered past sucking the air and leaving a hot diesel blast behind them. Tarmac slapped under their feet, Rosemary's single stick tap tapped, barely audible through the traffic. Dominic's sweat dripped off his face.

'It says we have to walk under the motorway via a storm drain.'

Dominic was sceptical.

'I'm sure that must be it. Worth a look if it means eight kilometres less beside this road.'

Dominic appeared to crumple on to a wall. Rosemary climbed down to the long tunnel that was wide enough to drive a tank through. She scrambled up the embankment at the other end and could see the fast moving river with the path, languid and shaded beside it.

'This is it,' her voice spiralled round the tunnel.

Dominic walked towards her through the gloom and out into the sunshine. His legs, black spindles against the light, detached from his body like pictures of African Bushmen blending with heat and landscape, finally reassembled.

The path widened to a tree-lined *rambla*, cool and quiet along the river to the very gates of Burgos. A cobbled street led to the cathedral square where they ordered coffee at a pavement café.

'Expensive,' Dominic said.

'Nice, though.'

Dominic put a handful of coins on the table by his cup, drained his coffee and stood. He picked up his bag and his stick and Rosemary looked up, expecting him to say something. He hesitated momentarily then walked away and disappeared into the quiet back ways of old Burgos and did not look back. She watched, unable to account for the

112

abruptness of the parting. She felt discarded like the ugly chocolate wrappers she'd seen cyclists drop. She went to sit a while in the quiet of a church just off the main square, where stout ladies dressed in black were on their knees praying. A soft sibilance came from their fast moving lips and the beads of their rosaries ticked away, out of sync one with the other as if time had no relevance there.

The church was quite plain, huge granite blocks heaving heavenward with barely any ornamentation. Even the alter was muted, no gothic splendour or baroque opulence. This was a humble church. She wondered why the ladies chose this church rather than the nearby cathedral with many more statues and treasures to venerate. Perhaps it was simplicity they craved to bring them nearer to the God they prayed to. Perhaps she should pray; for the world and for peace.

She had sat in an empty church in Clapham in the early days of her marriage and cried; tumbling out of the flat with tears streaming down her face and, too embarrassed, had ducked into the church thinking to find solitude. A young priest had come and asked why she was crying.

A confession.

How many times, my child? Priests always ask that as if that made a difference. As if *I killed a man, but only once* would be easier to forgive.

Do you love your husband?

Yes father. That is what makes it hard.

Does your husband love you?

Can you not see the flecks of scorn on my body? He sees right through me.

Does your husband beat you?

No Father.

Then what have you to cry about? For your

113

penance you must wear the sackcloth and walk on your knees until either you or he comes to your senses. And be sure to say a Hail Mary for me.

Yes Father.

Does your mother not tell you to get down on your knees and thank heaven fasting for the love of a good man?

No Father, I mean yes Father.

She had been unable to tell the priest, 'I'm a big baby, crying because marriage is not what I thought it should be. Life is a disappointment; I feel loveless, alone and trapped.'

Just as she had known that she was too old to feel sorry for herself. Perhaps if she had spoken to the priest he would have said, 'Meet me tonight and I'll show you loveless, alone and living on the streets.'

And she could have worked in his soup kitchen and done something worthy. As it was, she had carried on as before, finding that marriage was not a joy and that neither was she selflessly devoted.

Perhaps, if she had said something to Dominic along the lines: 'Hey, at least say sayonara,' he would have said, 'Good luck with your walk. Good luck with your life.' And that would have been that. She never said anything.

She escaped in to the sunshine, walking till she was clear of the busy city, towards arid fields baked hard for lack of rain.

SEVENTEEN

On the outskirts of Burgos in a leafy square lined with genteel houses there were two sets of yellow arrows. One set of hand painted signs advertised a hostel four kilometres further on, the other pointed in an opposite direction across fields of green leafy vegetables. Stefan consulted Dominic's list of the hostels. The names were only similar, not exactly the same. It could be an error on Dominic's part; it could be two different hostels. What would be the likelihood of Dominic *deliberately* getting it wrong? He had played that trick before. Stefan paced up and down hoping for a solution. He certainly did not want to walk four kilometres in the wrong direction, plus four kilometres back.

Rosemary appeared beside him without him having seen her arrive.

'Let me look at your guide will you?'

'Hello, Stefan, I'm fine thanks.'

Stefan looked at her from under his flop of hair to see if she was smiling.

'I know that, I just need to check something.'

'Sure.'

She whipped the little green book from where it was tucked into her waistband and handed it over.

'The arrows are confusing here.'

Rosemary nodded straight ahead.

'That's the path, I think. This just goes to a hostel. Four K is too far off the path just for a hostel.'

Stefan was convinced. They walked together, amicable and easy for hours till, tired and dusty at about four pm, they arrived in a shady village. Rosemary decided to stay. She had started walking at seven that morning and didn't think she could walk two more hours to the next place that Stefan named as his destination.

Stefan stood beside her while her *credencial* was stamped and her details entered in the log. He was sorry that he would have to walk the last stretch on his own. He lingered outside on an ornamental bench under an old oak tree and smoked a cigarette and was surprised when he saw Rosemary rush out of the hostel with her bag.

'I've crossed my name off the list,' she said and then burst in to tears. Stefan understood tears; and believed that much was achieved by shedding them. He envied women the facility. He let Rosemary cry for a few delicate moments, then he unwrapped the treasures he had purchased in Burgos: chocolate covered doughnuts, apples, cheese and sweet almonds. The sight and smell produced a weak smile from Rosemary. The first doughnut she ate thoughtfully, as if savouring every mouthful, then she said, 'I said goodbye to Dominic today, and I just couldn't face saying goodbye to you too.'

They ate everything, drank their water and felt merry again.

'Mind if I come with you where you're going?'

'Be my guest.'

Sometimes Stefan walked ahead and Rosemary walked in his shadow as it reached behind. Several times he turned to check on her. Sometimes she would take the lead and would turn to see Stefan as if asleep on his feet. Even as the sun slid lower and their shadows grew longer they did not lose touch.

They walked on, forty kilometres on one of the hottest of afternoons, over landscape so bleak it had its own beauty, the quiet and emptiness of a desert, or the moon.

It was dusk when they arrived outside the hostel. Dominic sat on the steps at the entrance, legs outstretched.

'What kept you?' he said. 'Ten more minutes and you'd have been too late to eat.' Stefan collapsed next to Dominic with a sigh.

As Rosemary started to climb the steps he said, 'Get a move on and we'll wait for you.'

'You go ahead; I'll join you later.'

'There is no later, they're serving now, give or take.'

They allowed her five minutes, after that they would keep a place for her if they could.

'They're strict here,' Dominic said intending the information for Rosemary, but she had gone. Stefan shrugged.

'She cried today,' Stefan jerked his thumb up the steps to the door, and Dominic shrugged.

'Is that what held you up?'

'No, not really. We're not all Flying Dutchmen.'

Dominic laughed and clapped his arm round Stefan's shoulders.

'So, tell me.'

'I took your advice and haven't written a message for two days. I haven't received anything either.'

'But that's good. It will get easier.'

Stefan considered this advice for a moment. 'I could kill a beer.'

Dominic nodded. He had already had a couple.

'I'll finish my cigarette and then see you there.'

EIGHTEEN

The hostel was an old house. Like the tardis, it was far bigger inside than it appeared from the street. Room after room rambled back, up steps, down steps. Successive rooms leading one into another had the oppressive feel of a tunnel burrowing deeper underground. Rosemary found an empty bed and bounced up and down to test if the mattress sagged, 'Not bad,' she said aloud in the room she thought was empty. Voices came from an alcove and she recognised the measured drone of dictaphone man and his companion. They were not visible and not quite audible, but it seemed to be a domestic scene and not remotely to do with bliss; the tone unmistakably disgruntled.

She imagined the woman saying, 'You never take the least bit of notice. You're always talking to your damn machine. Why did you bother asking me to come? To wash your socks for you?'

But she couldn't be sure. It was all part of the rich Camino Show. She tiptoed out of the room, feeling sorry for the couple that there was nowhere to argue in private. The Camino was anything but private, but the solitude of walking made it bearable.

It would be hard to factor in an argument stop: 'How often do you want? We could book in to a bed and breakfast every fourth day, if you think that would cover it.'

She shuddered at the thought.

'The Camino?' her son had said, 'isn't that for saddos?'

Rosemary had laughed, 'Do you mean me?'

It was his turn to laugh; only he didn't; he looked at her accusingly, 'Anyway, it's a bit tight on me Dad.'

She had not tried to explain. What could she have said? *Perhaps when you have more experience of life you will see a bigger picture.* That would have gone well.

Dominic was still outside when she came down the steps. He was stubbing out a cigarette when he saw her.

'Stefan is,' and Dominic trailed off and stood up straight away so even had she wanted to kiss him affectionately on the cheek he was out of reach. He led the way through the village to the bar where the meal was to be served.

'It really cost Stefan to get here; I could see it in his face.'

Dominic made it sound as though she had coerced him.

'I think he was looking for you.'

Dominic nodded, 'I wish I could help him; he's a bit insane.'

'There is still hope and I think you do help him. *He* certainly thinks so or he wouldn't have walked so far to find you.'

'Has he told you of his strange bargain? A pact he made with himself.'

Rosemary shook her head, 'No.'

'He is besotted with a woman who won't give him houseroom and has been for a decade. He is trying to give her up with each kilometre he walks. He's allowing a hundred.'

Rosemary was not quite able to imagine it.

'Why doesn't he?' she did not finish the sentence. Find someone else? Get over it? Dedicate his life to something? She knew it was not that easy. Short of joining the army there were not many complete changes of lifestyle. Walking the Camino, perhaps? But that was only a reprieve.

They strolled between mellow stone houses still

119

exuding heat, through narrow streets just wide enough for a couple of horses. Dominic pushed open the door to the bar and let Rosemary pass.

'Isn't Stefan going to eat?'

'He came ahead for a beer.'

The meal was festive. Dominic was cheerful and didn't mention his earlier abrupt departure. Rosemary was worried that he might feel his style was being cramped, but didn't mention it either. They sat at a table with a group of distinguished looking women. Tall and fine featured with boyish hair that accentuated large eyes, they flirted with Dominic in a witty and distinctly well educated fashion. Conversation sparkled. The Flying Dutchman was fêted that night in the intimate room. He was lord of all and Rosemary imagined that was how it was for him at home with his family. Windows steamed, more carafes of wine were delivered to tables. All it needed was music or singing and dancing to start up. The cook crept out, enticed by the jollity. Even his wife gave up clearing away and sat at the table, repeatedly wiping her thickened fingers on her apron as if she was nervous and allowed herself a glass or two of wine.

Faces were rosy and the laughter was good. Stefan enjoyed himself, growing more enthusiastic with each glass of wine. Rosemary quietly left, her eyes heavy, her body weary and her ankles worryingly painful. She negotiated the tunnels of the house till she came to her chosen bed near the window, which overlooked the entrance, and found that someone else had gone to sleep in it or were doing a very good impression. She felt like baby bear, but she did not squeak. The other beds were all occupied or saved with rucksacks. Her rucksack had been moved and leant against a wall. She remembered the alcove where the argument had raged and when she checked was relieved to find one of the four beds unaccounted for.

Sleep was instantaneous but not untroubled. The rhythmic sound of bed springs reaching a crescendo woke her up and possibly everyone else in the dormitory. With the final rallentando and a noisy trip to the bathroom allowing doors to bang, the couple went to sleep. She was not sure which emotion kept her awake: possibly disgust, but then she could imagine who one of the couple was.

In the morning Dominic was surfacing just as she was about to leave.

'Where are you heading today?' she was breezy.

He was reluctant to answer; he closed his eyes; perhaps he was imagining her dogging his footsteps all the way to Santiago, hoping she would go away.

'Give me your book,' he looked stern, working the muscles of his jaw, reigning in what he really wanted to say. Flicking the worn pages he jabbed at a hostel. 'Here. I'll be here tonight.'

'Oh, that's great,' she said without a trace of irony and took the book back to tuck it in the waistband of her bum bag.

She turned and breathed to herself, 'Just so I can be sure we don't meet up.'

Every time her mind strayed to the noises of the night, colour rose hotly to her cheeks and swear words flooded her veins. She resorted to walking with her eyes closed for ten paces at a time to alter her concentration.

NINETEEN

Stefan crouched beside the road struggling with a tin of sardines he was trying to open. The rich oil spilled on the road and he cursed. The curses subsided to a sigh as he finally managed to open the tin only for its contents to flip into the road. He sat back and gazed at the cluster of houses in the distance; a small town perched high and dome shaped on a hill, complete with red roofs and church tower. The path led straight to it with Roman precision, but Stefan was not certain he wanted to arrive at a small town so soon. He liked it in the semi wilderness. Except for the village they had stayed in the night before and isolated refuges, there was nothing for miles. The refuges were mostly ruined churches and so many of them along this stretch that he could not make up his mind where to stay. He had walked a mere six kilometres and his feet hurt. It was half past nine in the morning, he had not slept well and needed a gentle day after the forty kilometres the day before. Rosemary came up so quietly she made him jump.

'You didn't get very far,' she said

Stefan grunted.

'Weren't you kept awake last night?'

'No.'

He looked carefully at her from under his blond flop of hair.

'You must have heard something.'

Again she denied it and Stefan prodded the limp fish lying in the dust with the toe of his boot.

'I thought it was Dominic and some girl fooling around. He's an animal.'

Rosemary shrugged, 'He isn't that bad.'

Stefan spluttered, 'Fucking impossible,' and they

both laughed.

Stefan wanted to take a look at some of the refuges and asked Rosemary if she would join him. For a moment she considered the options: alone, because there were many miles to go without adding detours, or with Stefan, whose languor was anathema. The daily quota of miles she set herself was accomplished with missionary zeal. It was important to her sense of achievement to walk the entire five hundred miles; failure filled her with dread. Painful shins had replaced the blisters and the prediction that she would go lame was beginning to worry her. She was tired too; kept awake by the sound of heavy petting and the unkind stabs of jealousy. She smiled at Stefan, 'Ok, I'll come.'

His smile was ample compensation.

One of the refuges mentioned a pool for bathing, which sounded enticing, but when they arrived they saw concrete steps descend into green depths and layers of toads. At the next place, tucked out of sight, the refuge had been set under a brand new blue canvas in the ruins of a monastery.

The *hospitalero* was seated at a new camping table quietly reading a huge book, an illustrated monk's breviary or songbook. He looked up and smiled benignly when Stefan asked to inspect the tent. The bunks were new too. Stefan whistled his approval. Through the Perspex windows the ruins of a tower were twisted in the bright sunshine as if waiting for Van Gogh to paint them. Crows started into the blue sky and for Rosemary the peace of the place was overshadowed with thoughts of horror films.

'Fantastic.' Stefan produced his prism and squinted up at the ruins, measuring the light.

'This is where I'm spending the night, out under the stars beside the ruins.'

He tried in vain to persuade Rosemary.

'Will you wait for me while I register? I'll walk to the town with you; we can get a coffee or something to eat.'

She waited and they trundled into the little town of Castojeríz, half expecting cohorts to march up behind them on the straight road. Stefan was good company, showing a new side.

'I've been thinking about what you said about my polluted mind.'

'I shouldn't have,' Rosemary felt ashamed.

'You were right. I am a reformed character. Trying, anyway.'

'Jolly good.' And he laughed, as she hoped he would.

The first bar they found had tables set across the street under stunted trees that still provided blessed shade. Sandy coloured dogs lay anaesthetised in the middle of the street, occasionally cocking an ear. Stefan studied the blackboard outside the bar. The waiter brought red wine and bread and Stefan ordered.

'*Tapas*? What about omelette and some mushrooms with the dice of *jamón* and a scattering of parsley?'

Rosemary nodded and said, 'I thought perhaps you were making a horror film.'

Stefan pulled a ghoulish face and laughed.

'My film will fail miserably.'

'You can't know that. What's it about.'

'Love; doomed love, actually. It's about a man who is so in love with a girl who is not remotely interested that it drives him crazy.'

'This girl, the one in the film, is she worth it? Is she really so heartless? How does the film end?'

'I made several endings; one happy, where she

124

sees that someone so constant is a worthy lover, the others all end in disaster. Everything I have is mortgaged against this film. I gambled my life on it.'

She felt like hugging him. The hunch of his shoulders and the quiet of his voice out there under the trees; he was haunted by this woman, not the probable failure of the film, but the madness of love.

'Perhaps the worthy lover should choose a girl with a warmer heart. Perhaps he should cast his net wider or go on an odyssey.'

'I have walked the Camino before.' Stefan said. 'This time I am editing the walk like I would edit a film. Choosing locations for effect and selecting companions for what they will add to the whole.'

Rosemary studied the dogs. Not taking the rough with the smooth was an entirely new concept.

'Let me look at your guide book, will you.'

As Stefan studied her little green book, she wondered if it was her company or the book's that was adding to the whole. He took out a pencil and copied details.

'Don't suppose you want to part with this do you?'

She didn't answer; but wondered if she should forget her own agenda and keep him company under the stars. When he handed the book back she could see that he had retreated in to himself. She was too late to attempt such closeness. His blue eyes had a look of steel and all she saw was a tiny image of herself. Perhaps he had asked Dominic his advice; Dominic the good listener; and she hoped he had better advice from him.

Stefan leaned back, stretching his arms over his head, then stood up and helped her with her rucksack and kissed her cheek gently.

'Good luck.'

TWENTY

The path glittered as if enchanted and, after crossing a dried up river via an old stone bridge, veered sharp right and suddenly vertical. It was so steep that Rosemary stopped and laughed out loud thinking it must be a joke. All the pilgrims from the night before must have passed this way already. Dominic had perhaps jogged up with his latest paramour. Then she saw a man. He stood naked, except for sandals, and beckoning. A line of paper pinups, scantily clad women in lurid poses, was pinioned to the road with pebbles, leading to a shack that was no more than a jumble of boxes beside the road. The sound of an approaching pilgrim had perhaps enticed him out, but the laugh had caused him to slink away.

She pictured him in his lair, withdrawn to a corner in foetal position. His fantasies that he had displayed on the road, spurned by a thoughtless woman. There was something primordial in his display. It was also frighteningly bleak. Perhaps after a day in his lair airing his private parts, he simply collected his pictures, leaving a cairn of small stones, put on his suit and tie, picked up his briefcase and cycled home to a wife and 2.4 children. Perhaps this was another version of care in the community: all problems solved on the Camino: walk this way. Perhaps communities have always dealt with misfits by casting them out to work through their demons. They simply called them hermits and revered them as holy men who knew something about life.

She kept walking till the day grew overcast and stormy, climbing steeply most of the way till she reached blustery moor land and a crossroads. She felt like Jane Eyre fleeing Mr Rochester. Any moment a carriage and horses would draw up and the coachman would ask where it was she was going so late into the night. No carriage appeared, but in the distance she could see the ruins of another church. In her guidebook it described the hostel as decommissioned; semi derelict would have been more accurate.

When Rosemary arrived, flung back the door and prepared to fall through, the *hospitalero* barred her way with a false smile. He looked at her warily as if she was unreal, a spectre come to spoil the feast.

'There's another hostel in the village just two kilometres further, which would suit you better.'

She thought she had stumbled into purgatory, seeing heaving masses in the gloom behind him. There was more light in the dusk of the bleak moor than inside the church and more people inside the church than there had any right to be in so bleak a place. Why hadn't they all walked on? She had hoped, having walked forty kilometres to get there, for seclusion. She braved the wrath of the *hospitalero*; the thought of walking a step further was too awful to contemplate. Besides, the next hostel was where Dominic had said he would be.

After a meal, memorable only for the company of earnest young Germans, so ugly she did not want to look at them, and young Americans, so full of their career successes and wonderful lives that she did not want to listen, there was the highlight. The *hospitalero* prepared a *queimada*: a Galician tradition, a ritual burning; the origins of which are perhaps lost. He produced a bottle of luminous green alcohol and a small pot, quite charred on the outside, that resembled a caquelon used to make fondue. Pilgrims sprawled excitedly in a circle on the floor, on bags and cushions; the lights were minimal. The hospitalero poured vast amounts of alcohol into the bowl and set it alight; everyone was still but for a communal intake of breath. The sound heard at an auto da fé when the victim is condemned to be burned at the stake. It fell to the assembled pilgrims in turn to tell tales and secrets as the alcohol burned away, flickering on their upturned faces. It was quite a show, a Camino Show. Any moment Rosemary expected to be denounced. She had nothing she wanted to share, not even a joke. Fortunately the flames extinguished before her turn.

In almost complete darkness everyone settled to their sleeping arrangements. The *hospitalero* reluctantly led Rosemary to the altar where he assured her there was space. She picked her way looking for bare floor. Kittens darted about over recumbent bodies and their eyes glittered horribly.

There were just a couple of things that prevented murder. The first was a beautiful, middle-aged French woman, Murielle, sleeping in the next sleeping bag who offered her earplugs to drown out the mewling kittens. The second was a night trip to the outside lavatory in darkness that revealed the Milky Way: a silver panoply, leading due west.

TWENTY-ONE

In the morning, while all about them young people were busy with preparations for the day's walking, Murielle propped herself on an elbow, put on a pair of pince-nez and read by the light of a torch.

'We'd better get up,' Rosemary said.

'Why? Do you want to?'

'Not especially.'

'Well then.'

Murielle took a deep breath and called to the *hospitalero* in a rich contralto. Her voice soared the length of the nave, over the heads of astonished pilgrims, over worm-holed pews and the stone floor still marked with epitaphs, to where the *hospitalero* was putting steaming jugs of hot chocolate and coffee on the table. He did not sing back, but came rushing to see what was up. She asked him coquettishly for a lie in, *une grasse matinée*. Surely he would admit that she and her companion, indicating Rosemary, were old enough to be mothers to most, if not all, the pilgrims here? Perhaps even *his* mother? Surely he would grant his own mother a little luxurious lie in? Here she cast her wonderful gaze over the dilapidated surroundings with a hint of irony and a truly beautiful smile. Fortunately the young *hospitalero* was old enough to understand the ways of women and the French language. He gave in with grace and good humour; tempered by a modicum of strictness he might accord his own mother. They could stay till half eleven when he would have returned from his shopping errand. A moment longer and he would have to lock them in.

Fresh from the utilitarian showers, side by side with

Murielle in front of mirrors with rather mottled edges, they talked of philosophy and things of less consequence. Age and gender were perhaps all they had in common: both middle aged, both female. There the similarity ended. Murielle was tall, slender and blonde with an untroubled complexion, the result of a life of unrelieved pampering. The cool marble of her cheeks attained by wilting away hours under expensive creams and slices of cucumber; the grace and smoothness of her limbs arrived at by manipulation and professional epilators; sleek curls achieved in chic salons. She was without doubt the most utterly gorgeous creature ever seen, blessed by nature and the gods and magnanimous with her earplugs. Murielle had a studio, an atelier, in Lyons and yes, she could see the golden dome of the cathedral from her large windows.

Did she sell much work?

Pale blue eyes rested fleetingly, perhaps wondering at the crassness of the question and whether to answer. Then, with a voice that purred like a tamed jaguar, hinting at things exciting, sophisticated, unfathomable, 'I only do commissions, unless I am creating for myself.'

Lines furrowed Rosemary's brow, forced to contemplate an existence beyond her experience.

More comparisons were made: hours worked, hours slept, cars driven, flowers grown, relationships, boyfriends, mothers. Murielle spoke of lovers.

'It is good for the soul to take lovers. Do you have lovers?'

'Heavens, no.'

'But why not? You are not ugly. A little love. If you lived in my country…' Murielle moved her hands as if to say it would be inevitable, sighed wistfully.

'It is not love that is wrong, it is jealousy. I have

130

seen it many times in the faces of men.'

'I don't know many men,' Rosemary was thoughtful, 'but I expect I'd know jealousy, there are so many types.'

Murielle looked down, resting pale eyes briefly before seeing enough. This was the type of woman she loathed: provincial and frightened; a woman whose life was merely an extension of her husband's. She could see 2.4 children, a flabby waistline, an evening job for pin money, the ready smile like a door mat with 'you're welcome' written over it. She should make a statue that would be a wake up for women like this who existed all over France, all over the world probably, except it would be too boring. One gesture of kindness and the woman would stick like a limpet.

'You are married and have children? This is what you do in life.'

'It is what I have done, yes.'

Rosemary thought of expanding: I had dreams once; or, now that part of my life is over and I must lift my eyes, so to speak. She thought of the tears she shed into the echoing lonely house after the children had gone. Yes, she was branching out.

The subject of marriage was most illuminating.

'I chose this life,' Murielle was matter of fact. 'I could have married, but for me it was all art. I wanted a reputation for my work, but a reputation as a good lover can only help a career like mine. It makes men curious. It makes them want to buy my statues. They would like to marry me, but I am happy as I am. If I am happy why spoil it?'

Why indeed? A surge of admiration in homage to this self-commitment; it was an epiphany for Rosemary, that it was possible to live entirely for oneself and one's art. It was clear that nothing had

131

ever shaken the blessed one's firm belief that she was worth it; no inner voice had laid siege, no critical raised eyebrow deterred, no nagging little person had prior claim. Rosemary longed to touch the alabaster skin, to know if it was warm.

They left the hostel together when the sun was firmly established and those men and women who had monopolised sleep could be seen lumbering slowly across the horizon in a line like so many unearthly beasts.

The path wove through groves of trees whose straight barks stood in ranks, row after row, not unlike columns of soldiers standing to attention. Walking fast, the trees appeared to move, noiseless centurions tirelessly regrouping, so it was impossible to out walk them. Slowed to a stop, so did the trees. Murielle reclined a little off the path amid the silent silver soldiers, got out her notebook and began to sketch the trunks. The sinews of her jaw tightened as she worked. Rosemary wanted to watch her work. She took out a hard pear she had in her bag, sliced it carefully with her penknife and offered some to Murielle who looked up from her sketch and smiled as if she had not realised Rosemary was there. She declined the pear, '*La prochaine fois.*' Next time.

Every time Rosemary turned to look at Murielle she was engrossed in her drawing. Even as the path finally emerged from the trees she thought she could still see Murielle *la belle,* head bowed and wondered if she had fallen asleep. What would be the likelihood, Rosemary wondered, of meeting Murielle again? If she sat this long there would be no chance—unless she got a bus. Murielle didn't seem to care and appeared to leave everything to chance. Perhaps she believed in a divine meddler who would decide who should meet on which path and on which day.

TWENTY-TWO

Murielle breathed the warm wind of the moor land. It carried the scent of cistus and made her think of funerals. She passed a pilgrim lounged in heather like a solitary grouse. She felt tired enough to lunge into the heather and never get up, but was reluctant to admit she could go no further. Then a butterfly landed on the back of her hand, a delicate yellow butterfly like a ray of light. Its wings were edged with black dusting, like black pollen. Its body, tiny and fleshy, bristled with hairs. The butterfly, an object of loathing and childhood fear of being tangled in multiple black legs like probing fingers that once she would have instantly brushed off heedless of any damage caused, was allowed to linger for the first time and became an object of admiration. The wings closed like a book shutting its pages before all the words are read and it was gone; a mere hint of its presence lingered on her skin as gentle as an eyelash kiss. It did not stray far, an arm's length ahead, almost flirting; one yellow butterfly resting on cistus flowers that lined the path with a scent of incense. An omen? The Camino was a place for omens, shamans and charlatans on every stretch. One man's miracle is another's con trick, one man's prayers another's mumbo jumbo. The butterfly was an ephemeral thing, yet its presence made all things possible.

Murielle knew the time had come to dial the number her doctor had given her.

The phone rang and rang and just as she was about to give up it was answered brusquely, '*Dígame.*' She explained who she was and what she wanted.

133

There was silence, so long she thought the person at the other end must have grown tired of listening and quietly gone away, leaving the phone off the hook.

Then the voice said, 'Muriella?' A question, her name pronounced the Spanish way.

There was breathing in to the phone and muffled talking as if a hand had been placed over the receiver. She repeated the name of the next town and assumed he would deal with the rest. 'Mañana,' he said and she thought it a very Spanish answer.

Fromista: an optimistic name for a place not overburdened by its status as a Camino town. Not prosperous, not poor or pretentious; simply contented.

Murielle stepped down from the bus, bought a newspaper from a kiosk and wandered to a nearby café where she folded it; neatly hiding the headlines and threats of war, then laid it on a table before divesting herself of her bag. She ordered a cup of peppermint tea and took out the prescription that her doctor had given her and studied the name and address written on it: Padre Rafael Alonso Vasquez. She baulked at that idea of calling anyone Padre, Father, if they had no biological claim to the title. Rafael was a good name; an angel, and an artist.

When the tea came she sipped slowly, noting the tremor of her hands and thought of her degeneration, a natural process and a shame. Her life had been brilliant till now, lived con brio like a piano concerto whose cadenza falls at a furious pace. She took out a pencil and wrote several times under the name and address, in her measured, old-fashioned handwriting: *Murielle has been very lucky.*

'Mind if I join you?'

Stefan had already dumped his rucksack on a
134

chair and Murielle jumped. He bowed slightly when Murielle looked up and his blond fringe flopped forward.

Graciously she nodded. *'Je vous en pris.'*

'Bien?'

'Oui, tout est bien, merci.'

Stefan ordered a large espresso and a magnum, discussing in detail with the waiter exactly what he wanted, dark chocolate, with nuts, vanilla, but settling amicably for what was available. When the waiter brought his order Stefan stuck the ice cream in to his coffee and grinned at Murielle. He spotted Rosemary about to cross the main street and hallooed with a grand beckoning gesture. Even had Rosemary wanted to sneak by unnoticed, such a welcome could not easily be ignored. He introduced Murielle. Rosemary greeted Murielle warmly with kisses to either cheek. Then she lent and kissed Stefan.

'Don't want you to feel left out.'

Murielle looked for a translation, which Rosemary struggled to provide.

'That could be very useful,' Stefan said, 'The French. You know each other, then?'

Stefan lifted his magnum out of the espresso and alternately licked and sipped noisily.

'D'you think he'll let us have a taste?' Murielle giggled like a schoolgirl.

Stefan groaned, but stopped short of swearing.

'Murielle wanted to taste your ice cream, that's all.'

'That's different,' and Stefan would have summoned the waiter to order one for her, but Murielle stopped him. Stefan told Rosemary how lovely it had been under canvas and how fantastic the stars had been.

'You really missed out.'

'Got that right, Stefan, mostly it was hellish in the

135

ruined church. There was a *queimada*.' Murielle nodded enthusiastically, hearing the word.

'It was very beautiful.'

'I thought it was awful.' Rosemary confessed to Stefan.

Stefan shuddered, 'Camino show.'

Rosemary studied her guidebook.

'It says there's a doctor here in Fromista who doesn't mind pilgrims; I might get some advice about my ankles.' And she rolled down her socks to show them the inflammation. Murielle murmured in a conciliatory manner and placed cool fingers very gently on Rosemary's inflamed ankle. Stefan grimaced, a typical response, and asked to look at Murielle's newspaper, while the women still discussed the minor discomforts of long distance walking.

'What time is the surgery open?' Stefan looked over the paper at Rosemary.

'Now, actually.'

Stefan surprised her, getting to his feet,

'I'll come with you,'

When Rosemary explained that they were both going Murielle smiled,

'I don't need a doctor. I'll go to the hostel and see you later perhaps.'

The surgery smelt of disinfectant but there wasn't a queue. When Stefan and Rosemary were ushered in together the doctor looked up and smiled as if he was glad that he had someone new. He did not notice that they were sitting in on each other's consultations. Perhaps, since pilgrims must share intimate details of their lives with each other, he thought they would not mind. The doctor nodded benignly as Stefan told him about his blisters; invited Stefan onto the couch and gently put his feet in stirrups. They discussed a treatment, with Rosemary acting as translator when Stefan's Spanish gave out. To Rosemary the procedure sounded invasive and barbaric, but both Stefan and the medic deemed it utterly necessary for successful healing. The blisters were lanced, flushed with iodine and then had a wick inserted by means of an overlarge needle threaded through the skin. Stefan paled and closed his eyes tight shut for quite some moments unable even to utter his oath of choice. Then recovered sufficiently to thank the doctor profusely, who in turn modestly asked Stefan not to mention it.

The doctor turned to Rosemary who had the quick wit to deny all ailments, saying that she was merely accompanying her friend. The doctor, used to shysters, barked, 'Show me,' and she dared not refuse. He examined the swollen ankles, asked whether she could flex them and when she admitted that she could not, he declared her lame. Fortunately this was not a shooting offence for pilgrims, neither was there an immediate cure, but the medic warned against further attempts to walk thirty or forty kilometres at a stretch.

'This is the result.' He gave her painful, inflamed ankles a prod for good measure.

Murielle was sitting on the steps outside the hostel that was housed in a disused school when Rosemary and Stefan returned. The door had only just been unlocked to admit the day's pilgrims, so they entered and registered together. The hall was bright, spacious and clean. A group of teenagers manned the welcome desk, two of them efficiently asking pilgrims to enter their details in to a ledger; nationality, age and reasons for walking, (which Stefan left blank). Two or three others directed pilgrims to the stairs that lead to the dormitory, *El dormitorio está arriba*. Two or three more loitered, uncomfortable with their ill defined roles and scowled.

Upstairs opened to a wide landing like an atrium. A couple of doors led to former classrooms crammed with three tier bunks. Three tiers would guarantee minimum sleep; each occupant's circadian rhythm would cause the other two to shudder and shake with every toss and turn. However there were two adjacent single beds outside the fully bunked rooms. Even though they were in plain view of any and every pilgrim passing from bedroom to bathroom, to Murielle and Rosemary they represented an oasis of privacy. They eyed each other optimistically; realising that an opportunity for a quiet night might not present itself again and raced to claim a bed in the recognised manner: marking their territory with a rucksack. Seeing that he had been outdone, Stefan slunk toward one of the bedrooms.

'Ok, fine.'

And only when Murielle called after him to present him with a gift of earplugs and a smile and a kiss to either cheek, did he forgive the women for excluding him.

Then he was pleased to go with them to view a decommissioned church with the finest Romanesque capitals on the whole Camino and later to have a meal with the *patrona* fussing over them with the finest escallops to be found in Northern Spain.

Their farewells the following morning were warm; each believing that, with their different styles of walking, it might be the last and their friendship would become little more than a name they remembered in the pages of a register in a hostel.

TWENTY-THREE

Murielle sat on the steps of the hostel. It was closed. She had been the last to leave, the last to have breakfast amid the crumbs and spills of others. She simply waited. Too distracted to read or draw, she let her mind wander over the near past and the delights of the walk and fellow pilgrims and further afield to corners of her childhood. In each memory the sun shone and love showered on her. She thought how lucky she had been.

A dusty black saloon turned in a wide semicircle in front of the steps and beeped its horn. She had not asked her doctor anything about the priest whose name he had given her, and now she was curious. She watched him climb slowly from the car and come to stand by her. He said his name was Rafael.

Thin, almost gaunt, in a long black cassock that made him look even taller, with hands too large for him and an honest face. Murielle saw an angel.

Murielle had slept with the motion of the car. When it stopped with a crunch of gravel she woke with a jolt. The car's headlights lit the stone facade of a country house and threw silver shadows across the trunks of a small orchard that lay to the side. When Rafael turned off the engine there was deep quiet and without the headlights the darkness was bleak. There were no stars or moonlight to say they were alive, just the sweet smell of jasmine. Rafael got out and reached for her bag that he had placed on the back seat. '*Viene,*' he said, and motioned for her to follow. He put the bag on his back and even though it was not heavy, Murielle felt embarrassed that an old man should carry it for her. It contained her sleeping bag, a change of clothes a large pad of paper and a box of pencils; all that she had brought.

She heard the sound of a key grating in the lock and Rafael had swung the door open and reached inside to switch on the light with a click. Rather than illuminate the room, the light threw shadows across the stone floor. Gradually she grew accustomed to the gloom. Rafael placed the enormous key on the edge of a long, wooden sideboard. 'I am key,' it all but announced, 'Draw me.' She could imagine the cold weight in her hand and having to turn her pencil obliquely to achieve the desired shading.

Rafael stood close to her. He looked as if he had something pressing to say that he was struggling to keep in, but he didn't speak. She thought he might fold her in his long arms, but he didn't. He took her elbow and guided her upstairs to a bedroom, simple but adequate with a bed a table and a chair. He placed her bag on the rush seat of the chair and leant his hands on the back of it and they stood for a few moments looking at one another. His bright, pale eyes lingered on her face but did not scrutinise. He seemed far away yet reluctant to leave. She wondered if angels were ever lost for words. When finally he spoke, '*Casa*,' deep like a rumble, she did not reply, uncertain whether he meant she should make herself at home. He said it again more slowly, letting the word fall naturally in half. '*Ca sa.*' This time he made a sign for telephone and she understood. She shook her head. No, she did not want to ring home. She was not ready for words, not sure her voice would be steady. What would she say? That she had reached the end of the road? Besides there was no one she wished to tell. Jacques would fuss and she did not feel strong enough to support him. This was a challenge that needed her undivided attention.

140

Rafael's white hands began to flutter like a pair of love doves. She was mesmerised. He mimed eating and when she nodded in agreement he smiled fleetingly before lumbering to the door, which he closed behind him.

Murielle sat on the bed and stroked the white sheets, surprised how crisp and starched they were. She liked the emptiness of the room; it was peaceful. The black square of the window in the white uneven wall showed her reflection. She turned her head to look at herself in profile and a crucifix above the bed caught her eye; ceramic and brightly painted in the style of the twelfth century, although obviously contemporary. She reached for her pencils, shaking them out of the box and choosing one with a sharp point. She took out her drawing pad and smoothed her hand over the warm vellum. The pencil scraped over the blank page and for a while she was lost in concentration. She stopped, suddenly exhausted. Tears fell and she brushed them away with the back of her hand. She had replaced the humble face on the crucifix that had inspired her, with her own. She was angered by self-pity, but seized by the fear that she would lose everything she had in life and had taken for granted: dignity, beauty, reason.

Two rooms in the house would pass muster as private bedrooms. Rafael had been alternating between them, living out of his suitcase, awaiting the arrival of the French woman. One room, the one he gave up to her, had a fresh lick of paint and its own bathroom with hot water. Rafael had added a ceramic crucifix above the bed and a small vase of wild flowers he had picked especially. The other room that the last *hospitalero* was supposed to have finished had a hole and a large pile of plaster where there should have been a wardrobe.

There were things that Rafael knew about the sick and small things that he knew about women; both needed a degree of comfort and privacy. He assumed a sick woman would need these to a larger degree and should not have to suffer the indignity of sleeping with strangers on the bare floor.

Rafael did not know details of her illness. Dr Ernesto, the son of his friend, had not mentioned those, only a matter of time and that he knew he could be counted on, Good old Rafael. The 'old' was certainly true now; the 'good' he could only hope and strive for. Who would have thought two boyhood friends, whom life and the politics of their parents had contrived to separate, would have kept in touch for so many years? His friend had escaped to France at the end of the civil war and lived in exile, becoming a doctor and taking a French wife who had borne him a son to take over the country practice. Rafael had been called to the priesthood and lived contented enough under the old regime. There had been contact, but they had never seen each other again.

He had been afraid, when Dr. Ernesto had told him about Murielle, that he would be unable to help simply because he did not speak French and it turned out she did not speak Spanish. How could he help if they had no language in common? He had felt it keenly: a man whose life's work depended on words. It was indispensable that his advice to pilgrims, his sermons and homilies were understood. The Lord would provide, he assumed. He smiled as he remembered his terse attempts to converse, but the French woman had understood his mime well enough. He remembered the emphatic bounce of her blond curls when he had asked if she wanted to telephone anybody. Surely, such a beautiful woman did not live alone.

He wandered outside to pick fresh vegetables and instead sat on his favourite bench in the cool of the gentle evening. A bench rescued from the convent in the hamlet that used to house a community of nuns. Pity they had gone. They would have been more suitable for her. He turned his gardening knife in his hands and still did not move.

Rafael had walked the Camino several times in his life and had always looked forward to it, sometimes alone with his thoughts, sometimes as leader of groups of parishioners and students. Each time it had been meaningful and entirely different. Even the humblest of villages had revealed some new truth, some gem of architecture, some new prayer, some memorable person. There was much still to uncover, he was sure, but now he waited for truths to come to him and had hung up his boots.

He shared his table and the rather meagre pickings from his garden with his pilgrims. Some evenings the house was full of them, a dozen or more. They would start to arrive any time after four in the afternoon and would appear in the garden like new flowers sprouted amid the old fruit trees. He sometimes thought of himself as God's gardener whose job it was to cultivate these flowers, bring them into the house, bunch them together, cross pollinate them with fresh ideas, collect seeds from them. There would often be an influx of cyclists late at night. Rafael did not approve of cyclists, not on the Camino at any rate. What he objected to was their speed. It was as if they were cheating with their expensive machines. The Camino was a place for mindfulness and reflection; the rhythmic *plock* of sticks and boots, the body in tune with nature.

143

Cyclists always arrived too late for his little homilies, too late to contribute to the preparation of the meal, (seldom too late to share it, though). He always advised them to leave their bikes and walk and they always protested they did not have time to do that. 'It is not a question of distance,' he always told them, 'You must make time.' He was grateful no one else had arrived yet.

Only in the summer was Raphael a *hospitalero*. In the summer he retreated to this hamlet and ministered to pilgrims. He opened up this house that he had helped to fund out of his regular earnings as lecturer. Part time. Semi retired, now. What he did not relish sharing were the sleeping quarters. When he'd had occasion to enter the sleeping dormitory, the scattering of sleeping bags did not make him feel green fingered after all. A dogs' home came to mind with the smells and stertorous breathing, even the amorous approaches of some. Now he made sure never to visit after lights out, so to speak. He showed the pilgrims their quarters and left them to it, except for Murielle.

'Oh dear,' he said aloud to no one, 'This won't get the meal.'

Rafael got slowly to his feet, weary from the journey and forgot about vegetables. He hadn't even laid the table when Murielle came quietly to stand beside him. He could see that she had been crying. Frightened, he supposed, but also brave. He handed her a loaf of bread and a knife, 'Por favor.'

When she smiled, parting the perfect coral bow of her lips, Rafael was quite unprepared for the revelation of her pearly teeth. He was humbled, perhaps as the hunchback had felt in the presence of Esmeralda.

TWENTY-FOUR

Pilgrims live between worlds and have the best of both. For the duration of their time on the Camino they are responsible only to themselves. The bag of possessions they carry, symbolic of life and its concomitant burdens, which at first is too heavy to bear, becomes a mere nothing as shoulders strengthen and spirits soar. A pilgrim has only to accept what is freely given: an unwritten contract that only sometimes is requested, that the pilgrim will say a prayer for, or simply remember kindly, those who have helped them on their way. A sense of camaraderie prevails amongst pilgrims and great consideration, even respect, is shown by locals. Perhaps, because of this, the Camino is a place of healing, a place where good happens. It fosters a sense of well being, a sense that things will get better,

There was a coffee bar offering large slices of cake, an unusual offer, uncharacteristic in Spain even along the Camino and proving irresistible to vast numbers of pilgrims. Laughter billowed out, sending its message well ahead of the treat in store so that the weary walker, aware of some approaching spectacle, was curious to know what all the noise was about. The laughter followed long after too, so that any pilgrim who had not stopped retained the niggling sense that they should have.

Rosemary was one of the latter. An urgent pace, an inability to free herself from the cares she brought with her carried her past the glorious sight of people enjoying themselves. Two women who were sitting at a table nearest the path called out to her.

'You're always in such a darned hurry. Slow down

or you're going to miss all the fun,' one said.

'You can have this if you want it, we ordered way too much,' her companion chipped in as she caught Rosemary eyeing her cake.

Rosemary had seen these two before. She had tried to pass them on a slow climb where pilgrims toiled steeply uphill with their burdens like a column of ants and they had given her advice on how to walk and when it was advisable to rest. Rosemary had seethed inwardly and had not got past. It was inconceivable that anyone should attempt to storm ahead: the etiquette of the bottle-neck, they were ahead and she should keep her place. Conversation had been breathlessly attempted. They were Canadian nurses; one, a seasoned walker used to walking alone, had weakened under pressure and allowed her colleague to accompany her on this adventure. Even without breath, that first meeting, Rosemary had sensed the regret of her mistake. Rosemary had not wanted to stay close, privy to their intimate bickering, but had had no choice till finally the path levelled and broadened and she could stride out again and leave everyone safely behind till she had the path to herself.

A scent of fresh baking filled the air and her stomach lurched with longing for sweet cake, her shoulders sagged, her ankles throbbed; she relented and sat with the nurses.   The newcomer to adventures whose name was Mary Jean, was very smartly dressed in walking gear that rustled with newness every time she moved. She was never quiet. The old hand, Norma, dressed in a flowing black skirt down to her ankles, spoke less although she had far more to say. When she talked of walking way out in Canadian wilderness her eyes stared into distant stillness like a visionary.

Advice for her swollen ankles was offered generously but was conflicting. Mary Jean's bum bag (She called it her fanny pack which sounded vaguely obscene to Rosemary) crinkled with plastic bubbles of pills,

'Which should we give her, Norma, what do you think?'

Norma gave the impression that she was not listening, her eyes still fixed on the horizon. Her deep and throaty voice issued almost without moving her mouth,

'Not pills, Mary Jean, just rest.'

When Rosemary had finished their cake, which was light, lemony and delicious, and hoovered up the last crumb on a licked finger, Norma stood up and invited Rosemary to walk with them.

They rested frequently and for this day at least Rosemary adopted their pace. 'Slow and steady,' Norma eyed Rosemary's ankles, 'if you want to avoid injury.' When a vast haystack presented itself beside the path the nurses stopped without even consulting each other.

'A blessing like this is not to be passed up.' Mary Jean said, already fishing out her funnel.

'Oh my God what's that?' led to a discreet demonstration, the offer of the spare funnel to have a go and irrepressible giggling.

The haystack was as large as a barn yet, as far as the eye could see there was no dwelling, no stubble field, nowhere for the hay to have come from and no animals to benefit. They lay in its shade and dozed feeling the warmth from the bales, picking at the tightly packed straw to loosen some to chew, and wafting away insects.

When Rosemary woke up Norma was already standing by the path, gazing into the distance with her hand to her brow, her round knapsack on her back and a slight breeze lifting her skirt. Silhouetted in the early evening, she looked as timeless as the Camino itself.

In all the days that she had walked Rosemary had never met unkindness. Well, hardly ever. In one hostel a girl, who had been molested, turned on Rosemary as if it had been her fault, 'The Camino is not all *la vie en rose* that you seem to think.' Rosemary had not replied, but if she had she would have said she knew that, perfectly well, but nothing would stop her expecting the best of all possible worlds.

In fields just beyond a pleasant village with roads of beaten earth, there was a refuge with an overflow of tents, spilling round it. A night under canvas was an attractive prospect. The tents, old army A frames, had nothing of the grandeur of the tents Stefan had found near Castrojeriz. There were no gothic ruins, but there was a pool where the river had been dammed; a quiet place where cool water sparkled in dappled shade. If nothing else, it would be good to bathe inflamed fetlocks and travel-weary feet.

Her bed for the night was not in one of the tents. The *hospitalero* had refused her request because she was female and the other occupants were male. Her bed was as she had come to expect: in a small dark dormitory full of bunks and strangers making their preparations for the night and the following day's walk. One group were comparing equipment, one with another. A young man drew Rosemary into the discussion. Seeing her waterproof clothing neatly folded on the bed, he picked it up and weighed it in his hand, giving his companions a floorshow of how heavy he considered her jacket and trousers.

'Do they keep you dry?' She was on trial.

Torquemada was giving her a chance to redeem or condemn herself. His thin smile suggested that the entire walk, if not her future, depended on the answer and that he would not be held responsible if she got the answer wrong.

'Not particularly.'

He knew it. With a triumphant fling he replaced her possessions and then passed sentence: since she was the only female in the room it would be more appropriate if she went to sleep elsewhere. From the depths of a sleeping bag, someone groaned, 'Leave her alone, man.'

Rosemary left the room, hoping that the inquisitor would be asleep when she got back. She met up with the Canadian nurses who invited her to join them for a drink in the village. She was, as she suspected, a buffer for the bickering. Together they inspected several establishments. No matter what was on offer one or other of the nurses had an objection.

TWENTY-FIVE

A day of drenching rain; Rosemary had been lucky so far. She had an umbrella, an anorak, another ten miles and rain rolling down her neck on the inside. Her feet squelched in sandals. She watched pilgrims with rather dry smiles and their feet encased in stout waterproof boots, as they struggled to pull long ponchos over themselves and their rucksacks. They became a bevy of hunchbacks lumbering across the path, mythological beasts of apocalypse in driving rain.

She needed respite; here in the middle of nowhere she willed a café to appear and offer something hot to sustain and preferably, a roaring open fire to sit beside. Time and again other pilgrims said that the Camino was a place for miracles. When a distant neon sign broke the gloom she assumed it was a mirage rather than a miracle, although she was definitely on the outskirts of somewhere not mentioned in the book and she hardly dared hope it would be her heart's desire.

The windows of the café ran with condensation and a noise like a football crowd at a bad match exploded through the door. Of all the bars in the world the whole world was inside that bar. Old boys played dominoes, their heads conspiratorially close; small children trundled tricycles, annoying their grandparents; women argued, their belligerent body language the only sign above the din. All froze in a Breugel moment as she stepped inside. Here the remains of a community slowly curdled after the youth had been creamed off to work in the city, a mere ten miles away. Their dark, momentary stare betrayed scorn after the initial curiosity: 'only a pilgrim and a wet one at that. What on earth does she want to put herself through this for and why can't she stay indoors like decent people?' There was no sympathy. The quiet subsided, replaced by a trickle then a flood, enough noise to drown in. The bartender's eyes met hers over the bent heads of domino players in a mute exchange conveying an order for potato omelette and coffee and don't drip on my floor; there's a seat in the corner.

The nation that lives outdoors, congratulating itself for its good fortune and good weather, did not take kindly to rain and forced confinement. This community had moved en masse to the small bar to enjoy their misfortune together. It didn't rain often, but when it did Spain suffered a sea change, but not rich and strange. The sparkle went and it wasn't just the countryside: gone the languorous smiles and witty banter, in their stead, impatience and scowls.

She sat at an angle to the television, focused on its large screen and, as rain dripped from her in little pools on the floor and her coffee steamed like a magic potion in her cupped hands, she tried to blend in. An old boy approached the total exclusion zone round her table-for-one, shuffling on life-stiff legs, no longer quite patent, and stood expectantly. She assumed he was the spokesperson, the expendable fall guy, as happened in small communities the world over. There would undoubtedly be a pecking order: some village elder might be sent to interrogate an important looking male; a similar consideration might be afforded a young woman dependent on a sliding scale of how pretty she was. Here was Dimitri. Dimitri? But that's a Greek name. How on earth had he ended up with a name like Dimitri in this most Spanish of Spanish hamlets? He shrugged. He was not under investigation. The two-word dialogue seemed to satisfy.

'German?'

'English'

Drawing breath through his few remaining loose teeth with a whooshing sound he shuffled away to relay his information, lilting through the room. His hands brown and gnarled, dangled like dead twigs by his side. 'Ey Dimitri' the call from several tables.

A commotion started with the television. 'Turn it up. It's the news; we should hear this.' and the news was of Iraq; war with Iraq, a far off country with troubles that would make all others pale to rightful insignificance. The news jarred the room; Britain had joined the 'coalition of the willing,' and was committing troops. Not only was it a disgrace, they decided, it was unlawful. There were a few loud 'Shhh,' and clicking of tongues. Voices were momentarily lowered and eyes slithered towards the English zone in the café. Then the whole situation threatened to implode. At last, here was a real cause to brighten the day. Chairs scraped back, small stout men with ruddy faces were on their rope soled feet squaring up to each other.

'England is a belligerent nation, militaristic!'

'Small nation, small dicks, always got to prove something.'

'It's the Americans, you son of a.'

With the personal turn to the dialogue, suspecting a settling of old scores perhaps, one of the neatly coiffed ladies in black shoved a child and its tricycle hard towards the men's shins, hitting one square on. The argument stopped dead. Alternately rubbing his shins and looking accusingly at the old woman, he grumbled, *'Pero bueno, Mayka. En qué estas pensando?'*

Before she could explain, while one shoulder was still raised in a nonchalant shrug, the child toppled

152

off his tricycle and started to wail. That successfully trumped the argument, the news, and the rain. Everyone rose to comfort the child, lifting him up, passing him from one stout bosom to the next till his tears subsided and they were all rewarded with a smile.

The entrance of more villagers provided another diversion and she prepared for a quiet, but hasty, retreat as she scooped up the last of her omelette and stuffed her possessions back into the rucksack. In the doorway she looked back to see the new arrivals stepping round the pools she had made as if they were her bodily excretions.

It was still raining and there were still ten miles to walk; ten miles on an omelette. She was stung by the truth in the argument of the illegality of war. She thought of soldiers, young boys too green to know that war is never glorious and never just. What had happened to the old lie? When had it been decided that, after all, it was sweetly just to doom youth to die for their country?

The hostel in Leon was full by the time she arrived and she was directed to a convent deep in the medieval streets near the cathedral. That was full too. The nun who finally answered the clanging bell, echoing inside the convent, apologised that there were just no beds left: a saturation point had been reached. Luckily Rosemary could not summon the Spanish for, 'Bloody hell, woman, can't you see I'm way beyond it myself?'

When the nun offered her a place on the floor of the adjacent school gymnasium, she nearly kissed her.

She stripped off all her wet clothes and lay shivering in her sleeping bag on the cold floor, curling up on her back and rocking to and fro like a struggling tortoise.

153

For some time she lay like that, not interested in the room the size of an aircraft hangar or who she might recognise lolling amid the strewn sleeping bags, rucksacks, boots and plastic bags. The sight was reminiscent of news screens after some natural disaster and thousands of rescued people. Again she thought of war and may even have closed her eyes; sleep is a body's natural defence.

'You going to Mass tonight?' A foot was levelling with her thigh.

'Stefan.' She was overjoyed to see him. A surge of inexplicable joy.

'Well?'

She laughed at his impatience. He might have come straight from some exclusive men's salon.

'You look very clean,' she said.

'You don't.'

'What time's Mass? I've only just got here.'

'Don't make excuses; you've been asleep half an hour. You've got another half hour to get ready.'

'I thought you didn't believe in God.'

'I don't, but you never know in this life. Take you for a drink after.'

'Now you're talking. Will anywhere still be open?'

But he had turned on his heel with only a smile lingering over his shoulder.

The chapel was small and pilgrims and parishioners stood shoulder to shoulder. The nun's voices coming from behind a grill to the left of the chapel were sweet and wavering; old women's voices. Religion doesn't interest the young, she thought, yet this chapel was full of youngsters making a pilgrimage. And after Mass they spilled out through the door with thirst for life. Perhaps, just thirst. They were all in the little bar she and Stefan found still open.

154

Sleep with earplugs takes out more than the sense of hearing. It is another world; an eerie, total quiet, where things happen inconsequentially and without warning. However earplugs had afforded Rosemary a good night's sleep; a sleep of uninterrupted nightmares. She had dreamed of headless riders and bloated bodies of dead pilgrims in ditches and worst of all, that she would be unable to finish the walk because she was lame. On waking she slowly came to earth, gathering her wits and possessions, and prepared to leave, carefully stashing her earplugs. Her ankles throbbed, the skin, tight and inflamed. A couple of years before a similarly swollen ankle had led to serious illness and a week in hospital with intravenous antibiotics. Gripped with fear that she would not make it to Santiago she realised how much it mattered to walk the whole five hundred miles.

The nuns had prepared hot chocolate and bread for an astonishing number of pilgrims; five thousand, perhaps. It did not feel miraculous to Rosemary, merely frenetic. There was no sign of Stefan.

TWENTY-SIX

A long walk on tarmac amid heavy traffic finally gave way to a path over a heath starred with drifts of purple crocus. An abandoned house in an almost deserted village advertised itself as a hostel with a dilapidated sign. There was no *hospitalero*, not even a warden, to greet weary and foot sore pilgrims. A handwritten notice reminded pilgrims to sign in and asked for a contribution for much needed maintenance. As Rosemary flicked a couple of pages of the register she saw Dominic's name logged three nights before.

The hostel had an inner courtyard and a wooden balcony at first floor level that was completely full of sleeping bags. Most pilgrims who had opted for a night under the stars were young and still starry-eyed themselves. Rosemary wondered if Dominic had slept outside or if he had ended, without much choice, on a mattress on the floor in a damp room overrun with silverfish.

A group of young Germans who had been in the decommissioned church with the *qeimada,* who on first meeting had seemed too earnest for words, invited her to eat with them. Rosemary, tired and inclined to be tearful, was fortified by their generosity and was truly grateful. She was treated as a respected elder whether or not she deserved such distinction.

She slept-in the following morning, well after the young people had gone. They had left her a note in the kitchen wishing her *'Buen Camino,'* and inviting her to make use of the last of their coffee and bread. This time their generosity released the tears that she brushed away with the back of her hand; glad no one witnessed them.

She arrived at Hospital de Orbigo by mid-day and lingered on the magnificent medieval bridge. The narrow stone bridge was at least a mile long with twenty arches that kept curving way after the breadth of the river, perhaps to keep the traveller above dangerous marshes. Any moment there would be a fine procession of knights clopping over the stones on white chargers chinking in chain mail, bearing fluttering pennants. The marshes were now tightly planted with rows of slim poplars, *chopos*, the harvest of quick growing wood for the benefit of the town. Their seeds scattered like a snow scene on a film set or inside a glass bubble.

As she sat to eat her customary bread and cheese on a tiled bench in the village square, an old lady with a shopping trolley and a dog asked her if she was a pilgrim and if she was alone. When Rosemary admitted that she was both a pilgrim and alone, the old woman's face twisted in sadness, '*Ayee*,' followed by lengthy tutting. '*Pobrecita*.' Poor thing. It is not good to be alone.' Rosemary did not even attempt to explain that it had been her choice to come alone, nor that she would now agree with the woman's sentiment: it was not good to be alone.

All afternoon the woman's *Ayee* haunted her with its implication that living alone would bring sadness. Even after she arrived in Astorga, left her rucksack in a vast hostel almost buried in boots, and walked the remains of the town walls, there was no escaping the stigma or folly of choosing solitude. Gaudi's museum had only a whistle stop tour and the delightful interior only the briefest of glances. On the Camino the carapace, the rhythm of walking and assorted aches and pains, the beauty of the landscape, the wind and sun on her face left little time for melancholy. Only when she stopped did all thought

157

come, troublesome, and leaving her feeling truly alone.

When it was time to find somewhere to eat in the evening, she bumped in to José Luis.

'Ah, Rosa Maria.'

Perhaps he was going to eat?

He looked at his watch and looked at her as if she was mad, then made concession, remembering she was English. He had eaten *menu del día*, of course, over the midday and would not need to eat again. He described a huge merry meal, a speciality of the region with a group of Spaniards.

'It would have been wasted on you; you eat like a bird,' a good-natured accusation. Rosemary said that today she felt hungry enough to eat all the boots piled in the entrance and nodded at the mound. José Luis threw back his head and laughed, then lurched a little toward her.

'Remember Churchill.' And she could feel warmth radiate from his rosy cheeks. He straightened up and headed for his bunk and a little sleep.

TWENTY-SEVEN

Rafael felt blessed in Murielle's company. Her beauty visited him in his dreams, testing him. Even when Murielle was tucked away in her room, Rafael was aware of her, aware of the sound of her breath as she breathed with the house through the night and he listened at her door. He tended his garden, cleaned the house, cooked, filled his days with minutiae that usually left his mind free to write his sermons and yet he wrote nothing; he simply thought of her. That he should feel like this, as he had not felt since a young man suffering the first pangs of unrequited love, was a trial and a gift. Relieved of words, since she did not understand him, he established a new way to communicate. It had brought a closeness he had long forgotten was possible.

When Murielle began to search his house for brushes and old paint he had been enormously worried for her sanity. He had heard that those who suffered could undergo complete personality changes, even becoming violent. Murielle certainly set about emptying his cupboards with energy, only to bellow with frustration when the search proved fruitless, and he would follow her around tidying away, mystified. Eventually he snatched up her pencil and drawing paper and thrust them at her so she could draw what it was she needed. She laughed and laughed before feverishly sketching a list.

At first he had thought he was giving her strength, imagining that hers was ebbing slowly day-by-day. When she had begun to paint the whitewash of the outside wall with giant strokes and brilliant colours he had worried that she might break. On refelction he knew that it was Murielle who was supporting him. He felt humbled after so many years of sacrifice and celibacy, of dedicating his life to God that he might have been wrong.

Murielle was aware that the priest stared, but was not offended; rather, she was comforted as the gentle days passed. She attended his evening services for pilgrims, not understanding much, but aware of his voice and the humility of his gestures. Pilgrims came and went; Spanish, German, even Japanese, but for a whole week, never French. So Murielle never spoke, but participated simply by lending her smile. Until Dominic.

She noticed Dominic almost as soon as he arrived in Rafael's garden. He stood like an alien bloom, a giant dandelion clock sprouted head and shoulders taller than the other pilgrims with him.

'Here is a man,' she'd thought, knowing nothing of him, 'with a capacity and need for love.'

She wanted to draw him, capture him and preserve him as he seemed to her. He sat near her at the table for supper and spoke continuously in Dutch. The sound of his voice excited her and she longed to lie in his arms through the night and be comforted by him. It would be a symbolic act, an act of union, a celebration of life. He would be gone the following morning and no doubt would think nothing more about her. She thought of the fragile yellow butterfly leaving its delicate touch on her cheek.

Dominic contemplated his arrival at Rafael's: It could have been fated, it could have been his destiny. Whichever way he was glad. For several days he had not found pleasant company to walk with, being stuck, by force of circumstance, with a couple of Canadian nurses. Not that he had anything against Canadians or nurses. In fact one of them was interesting. Together they had been a nightmare of bickering. Their voices could be heard echoing on the empty plains or he would surprise them in pitched battles round quiet corners of the path. Worse, in the peace of a hostel they would ask other pilgrims to arbitrate or take sides. He had heard of Rafael, a priest and a healer, fond of classical music, who ran his hostel autocratically and had assumed he would be too much part of the Camino Show. He had fully decided to give the establishment a miss and walk the alternative mountain pass, but rather than risk having to walk or stay yet again with the nurses he had deliberately chosen a different path to theirs, the one that would inevitably lead to Rafael's hostel. When he saw the French woman he decided it was destiny.

The French woman was truly pretty. She sat beside him, which aided his digestion and enjoyment of the meal. He courted her with little attentions throughout and she rewarded him with a smile enough to set even a heart of stone fluttering. Her voice was essence of woman and very sexy and, although he did not understand a word, enticing. Murielle; he did not know anyone with that name. He liked the way she called him Dominique. She disappeared after the meal when Rafael made an announcement about the service in the church in the village and Dominic did not know where to find her.

He sat and thought about a prayer Rafael had encouraged them to write, not to be read that evening, but to form the basis of subsequent services, read by strangers. He supposed he could pray for his family; success for his play or simply give thanks to being alive and walking the Camino. He could give thanks for beautiful women.

Any doubts as to the validity of that prayer and whether or not God had a sense of humour were dispersed on entering the humble chapel; for there was the beautiful woman. Dominic went to sit beside her. She was kneeling with her head in her hands. He particularly liked the soft line at the back of her slender neck where her head bent forward. Dominic did not pray; he did not believe there was a higher being who listened. He reflected and he tried to be a good person. What else could be asked of a man?

Rafael handed out letters to be read during his service; letters left by others on previous days—prayers, supplications, petitions that he had encouraged them in their turn to write. Rafael selected the letters by language, according to those nationalities registered in the log. Those letters that would not be understood by anyone were left for another time.

When Rafael stopped at the bench where Dominic sat with Murielle he took Dominic's face in his hands and looked long into his eyes. It was as if the priest was blessing him. Dominic was inordinately touched by the gesture; and he wondered why the old priest had singled him out.

He scanned the letter Rafael had given him that had been left by a Dutch pilgrim some days before. The message was full of optimism for world peace and it made Dominic feel old and world-weary. He could imagine the earnest young man, most likely a teenager, who had written it and sighed. He would read with conviction, however, even though his were the only Dutch ears for the message. Perhaps just the disturbance of the air in the chapel would reverberate round the world and cause a ripple. That was the most he could hope for his plays after all.

When the service ended he followed Murielle noting where she went upstairs. He waited a short while and then went to find her room. Her door was left ajar and he closed it behind him. She turned to smile then turned back to gaze out of the window as if she had been expecting him.

Murielle woke as sun streaked through her window and danced on her eyes, around half past nine; about the time Rafael usually knocked lightly on her door to deliver breakfast to her on a tray; always a little jar of fresh flowers, freshly squeezed orange and dainty pieces of toast to dip into her coffee. This gentle greeting eased her into the day. Rafael would search her face for signs of pain and Murielle would return his look with such a bright smile he would be reassured. This morning there truly was no pain and no reassuring knock from Rafael.

'He knows,' she thought with a rueful smile.

Dominic had left her room very early, perhaps to sleep in his own bed, but he had stayed with her and she had been glad. Rafael could not object, surely?

She played her fingers over her lips, cradled her breasts still tender from the night before and felt uneasy. Her life was art and love, but she knew the wounds inflicted by jealousy. She thought of a life without sex, the celibate life of a priest. Perhaps even priests could be jealous. Had she been a fool? She had never been coquettish and had only sometimes revelled in her power over men. She shrugged, but she had the impression that she had broken some unwritten law between them.

She got up and looked out of her window from where there was a fine view of her artwork. Rafael usually stayed in the morning just long enough to gaze from her window. He never commented or

163

asked her about the huge mural. She hoped he would like it since it was a present for him. Already the colours, iridescent pinks, creams, blues, were pleasing and reminded her of a huge fluffy cloud. Even this morning, as the early promise turned to heavy rain, the colours sang out as she had hoped.

TWENTY-EIGHT

Several pilgrims arrived together in time for coffee in the first visible café in Ponferrada, crossing the metal bridge that gave the town its name, passing by a prominent Knights Templar castle with a distinct lack of curiosity. It was a festive, noisy group that had set off early without breakfast and had already walked twelve kilometres; swelling then gradually dispersing till Rosemary was the only one left, leaving the rather flat feeling of warm champagne the morning after. It would be a long walk to the next town with everyone well ahead and no chance of company. It made her sorry for herself, as if the task of walking all day alone was in preparation for the rest of life.

She was wrong about the pilgrims all being ahead. Stefan appeared and a day that at one moment had looked bleak and hard became delightful.

'I think I must have conjured up some Camino Magic,' she said.

'I'm not part of the show,' Stefan smiled.

'Where did you come from, then?'

But Stefan said it was pure coincidence that he had happened along.

They shared grapes picked from the fields, marvelled at tiny ornate churches nestled among the vines and walked and walked, further than was sensible. That original pain relief Rosemary had found in the early days—thinking of something else —worked till they neared the hostel in the early evening. They stopped, squatting at the roadside in the dust with their destination, Villa Franca, a huddle of tiny roofs in the distance. They had precious little water left and the dust caked their throats so that it was hard to talk. Rosemary remembered that she had an orange in her bag and they shared it. The juice exploded warm and sweet in their throats as the sun blistered their necks. The zest on her hands immediately clogged with dust and she groaned.

Stefan told her to cup her hands and poured the remains of his water into the perfect bowl and the sense of relief was intense, like expiation and absolution writ large in the vast dome of sky. 'It's no trouble,' Stefan said when she thanked him.

Zest: a life force that some have in abundance and cherish; that for others is no more than an uncomfortable sensation to be complained of. Once, Rosemary had heard a tour guide explaining that bitter oranges were simply ornamental. It was only the English who did not understand this and cooked the life out of them by making marmalade, a pale imitation of the real thing that they relished with their breakfast.

They arrived so late at the hostel that she climbed into her allotted bed as soon as it was shown her. She gave the briefest of nods to José Luis who happened to have a bed not too far away. When José Luis saw her he turned accusingly to the shrugging Stefan.

'What have you done to her?'

Rosemary was afraid Stefan would be rude, but he said nothing. José Luis looked down at her, 'You shouldn't have let him bully you into walking so far; it's not good. At the very least, you should have made him carry your bag for you.'

And the thought of a new kind of beast, one person under two great rucksacks, made them all laugh.

When it was time to go into town for an evening meal with Stefan and other pilgrims, Rosemary refused outright to walk another step. The *hospitalero's* daughter, from a family renowned for their

166

hospitality along the Camino, offered to make a sandwich with tomatoes from her own garden. José Luis, who had already eaten well that day, kept her company at a table in the courtyard and asked for red wine, which they shared. The wine made Rosemary shiver she was so tired.

The following day, when Stefan was up and ready, calling for Rosemary to walk with him, she was still in bed.

Perhaps something of the old melancholy lingered in the town. It was here that sick pilgrims, who would not live through the rigours of climbing mountains to reach Galicia, could end their walk and still receive their indulgence from the church that had its own *puerta del perdon*, a humble replica of the one to be found in Santiago. Their journey home would begin from here, if at all. Rosemary did not feel she was dying or that she was ready to give up, but her body, especially her ankles, cried for rest. The swollen fetlocks that the doctor had prodded had seized up, the shivering of the night before had not abated and she had no desire to push on hard through the mountains. The day had come when, devoid of energy, Rosemary could hardly walk.

She lounged about town, with only her rucksack for companion, coming to rest outside the church. Also lounging was an old man, the sort a rural community seems to produce, so gnarled by experience of life and so brown he could have been part of a vine. Without having to be asked, without questioning her circumstances, he advised her not to walk through the mountains.

'It is very beautiful, but very hard. Walk on the road and after 23 kilometres you will come to a hostel.'

Before she thought to thank him he had moved

167

off. Rosemary half expected bunches of grapes to fall in his wake. She flicked through the pages of her guidebook, but found no mention of this hostel. It was worth the risk; even a road less travelled would lead somewhere.

At a village dwarfed by a motorway flyover a large yellow arrow on the road pointed to the hostel, a stone house with a gravel drive and the remains of an orchard beside it. The door was open. A passage led ahead to a dining room with long tables beautifully and formally laid with little jars of flowers and pitchers of water and wine. Pilgrims were wedged in along the length of them till there did not seem room for anyone else. All froze on seeing the stranger at the door. After the long afternoon in meditative silence, Rosemary wondered if they were real or simply a painting, forever waiting for the meal. Then someone acknowledged her arrival and the scene erupted with a tumult of chatting.

'Just a minute,' a man appeared down the hallway carrying a large white soup tureen, which he placed on the nearest table as if it was very heavy.

'We will make room for you.'

He disappeared the way he had come and reappeared with another place setting in his hand. 'Yes, yes,' he said 'Leave your bag and sit here.' And she was squeezed in. Rosemary looked down the length of the table; at the far end, Stefan sat opposite Murielle; she tried and failed to catch their eye.

The *hospitalero* brought lighted candles, which gave the scene a magical feel. 'Nice,' he said, smiling in a fatherly way at the effect as he served the soup with a large ladle.

'Everything is from my garden,' he was proud of his soup.

Several pilgrims made complimentary comments about the soup,

'Rafael, you've excelled yourself;' or, 'what an exquisite taste.'

The soup certainly was unusual; it was pure white and cold.

'What do you think is in it?' he asked more than a few times.

'It tastes of apples with garlic and perhaps almonds,' Rosemary said and Rafael gave her a filthy look as if he really did not want anyone to guess the correct answer straight away.

After the meal, as the scent of joss sticks and a recording of Debussy filled the air, Stefan explained Rafael's game to her. Most nights Rafael quizzed his pilgrims about what was in the soup, but he did not want them to guess correctly. He wanted to finally relent and give the answer himself when all possibilities had been exhausted.

'So, you got here after all?'

'Thought you'd have gone the high, hard road, Stefan.'

'Not this time, I am being kind to myself. Besides, Rafael is a healer, the real McCoy. He's a bit famous on the Camino.'

'Do you think he would heal my ankles?'

Stefan gave her a hard look as if to say Rafael only dealt with deserving cases.

'He'll be here soon to ask you to write a prayer. He does a service every evening in the chapel. I was going to skip it tonight, but since you're here, I'll keep you company.'

'Thanks, Stefan.' She was touched.

'Murielle might be there. She's been staying a while.'

*

At first Rosemary thought everyone must have retired. Music had been turned off and the house was quiet but the smell of incense lingered. Doors leading off the main hall were closed and candles flickered. The pages of a book rustled and she spotted Rafael and went to disturb him. She asked the possibility of a bus for the morning as walking was all but impossible because of her ankles.

Rafael put down his book and glanced at her ankles over pince-nez. He asked her what languages she spoke; a non-sequitur, the relevance of which she did not appreciate. When she said that as well as her mother tongue and enough Spanish to get by, she also spoke French, he was suddenly attentive. There was no need to get the bus; she must stay and he would help her and then she could help him. A bargain. He told her to please wait a few moments; he wanted to get something. He stood, a tall man with a slight stoop, and padded on rope-soled shoes to one of the rooms off the hall. She looked at a photograph on the wall of Rafael several years younger with a group of teenagers. Before she could lift it down to look more closely Rafael had returned with a phial of round white pills like tiny pearls. His instructions were precise.

'Take two now, then in the morning, one every two hours; under the tongue, no crunching.'

When he was satisfied that she understood he wished her good night and picked up his book.

Such peace reigned in the house that Rosemary felt she should tiptoe. Once zipped in her sleeping bag she remembered her earplugs but was reluctant to get up again. There was no need for them; she slept till *Ride of the Valkyries* blasted out in the morning. Grateful that she did not have to muster,

170

she stayed in bed through Mozart's *Ave Verum* and half a piano concerto she did not recognise, before pulling on some clothes and going for a typical Camino breakfast. Pilgrim after pilgrim packed up and left.

The day inched forward. Rosemary struggled with the emptiness, alternately falling asleep in a hammock that hung between fruit trees in the wild garden or gently rocking it to the hum of bees and the occasional plod of feet and accompanying plock of sticks on the nearby lane. In a patch of wasteland opposite, an old woman (Dickens would aptly have called her a crone) was brewing something in a large blackened cauldron over a brazier. There was no wind to carry the smell. The woman's back was bent double as if buckled under a life of strain, yet, as she stirred, she sang softly to herself and to the chickens pecking around her in the dirt. Occasionally a cock crowed. Hours passed without effort as if life here was just something that happened, day after day, highs and lows inevitable as weather fronts.

The healing was offered in the afternoon; it was a laying-on of hands, without any actual touching. Rafael came to find her and asked her to follow him to his office: a small room with a desk, a chair, a library of books and a mattress on the floor.

'You lie back and make yourself comfortable; use the cushions.'

Rafael bent down at Rosemary's feet with the agility of a much younger man.

'You must relax,' he said.

She thought he might ask her to think of England and she would be consumed with giggles and that would never do. Rafael was serious and business like. His hands hovered over each ankle in turn.

171

'When you feel the heat you must begin to flex your feet.'

That did not seem a possibility with feet and ankles welded together.

The heat, when it came, was searing and for an instant Rosemary thought it would be unbearable. Instead, the pain stopped abruptly, the stiffness eased and with each movement the redness and swelling began to recede. She laughed in surprise. If only other cures were that simple, or perhaps they were.

Rafael did not want thanks or praise; he simply wanted her to go, and sent her into the garden to find Murielle.

Murielle sat on her haunches with a decorator's brush in her hand gazing at her wall. A scarf folded round her head made her look like a land girl from the 1940s. She half turned to see who was coming. The look in her eyes was the look often caught on camera in prisoner's eyes, not of death or fear but of defeat, the death of hope. Rosemary was not quick enough to hide her shock. In the days since they had last seen each other there had been a dramatic change. The beauty of the face was there, but when Murielle smiled the perfect teeth stood proud of her sunken lips in a rictus.

'How's the mural?' Rosemary asked.

When Murielle spoke of her painting she recovered and looked like the old Murielle, the artist with the atelier in Lyon and the fine view.

'Do you ever find that something that begins as duty, to please someone else, becomes in itself a pleasure?'

'Is that the meaning of your painting?' Rosemary struggled with the abstract before her.

'There is no meaning.'

They could see Rafael hurrying towards them,

172

through the garden; his manner was grave.

'Please will you tell Murielle that she has worked enough today.'

Rosemary duly translated; it seemed a reasonable observation. Murielle replied that the desire to finish the painting was keeping her alive, and Rosemary asked if she really wanted her to translate that.

'No, you're right,' she softened her tone. 'Ask him if he likes the mural.'

The day that had tended to be overcast, hanging round them like a sulky teenager unable to make up its mind, was suddenly gloriously sunny. The effect on Murielle and Rafael was equally dramatic. They smiled at each other and Rafael stood close to Murielle.

There was luminescence. Light emanated from the wall; ethereal like Murielle's skin. All eyes turned to the painting. Pilgrims with their staves and scallop shells that before were not discernible, now stood out as if in three dimensions; some in shorts, some dressed as monks, some in traditional peasant clothes, some with no clothes at all. All the pilgrims were sheltering under the giant wings of an angel and the result was beautiful.

The three were silent, looking from one to the other. The laugh started with Rafael; a chuckle at first then louder and helpless till tears streamed down his cheeks and he had to hold his ribs because the unaccustomed use of muscles was making them ache. Murielle laughed, as if the laugh had taken hold of her, till she was breathless and tears ran down her cheeks too. Rosemary felt her belly shake and ache with helpless and irrepressible laughter.

Pilgrims began to filter out of the house and gather in the garden. Everyone responded to Murielle's vision by laughing. Stefan was the only one

173

who did not laugh, but even he could not take his eyes off the picture.

When the laughter quietened no one could say why they had been so overcome with the urge to laugh. No one made a move, perhaps not wanting to miss another opportunity for such unbridled mirth should one be in the offing. They nodded to each other, smiling shyly, as if they had all been witness to each other's intimate idiosyncrasies, but were once again regaining control.

'I'd like to stay here for a while.' Stefan almost breathed the words, 'Will you ask Rafael if that's possible?'

'You like Murielle, don't you?' Rosemary said.

'I do, but that's not the reason. I want to stay near Rafael.'

'Rafael, Stefan would like to stay on and appreciate the peace of your house and garden and your company; would that be possible?'

The answer was not immediate; Rafael's breath was still wheezy from all the laughter. His eyes still scanned the picture as if he was reading.

'What are you saying, Rosemary?' Stefan stood like a schoolboy about to be sent down.

'I am pleading your case.'

'He can stay, of course.' Rafael said, adding, 'I must check my soup.'

He put his arms round Murielle and gave her a kiss on either cheek. He looked in to her eyes and held her for quite some moments.

'Thank you.'

Stefan volunteered to give Rafael a hand and he too gave Murielle a hug.

'That's some picture,' he said.

'You know,' Murielle began, when most pilgrims
174

had drifted away and she and Rosemary were alone again, 'Everything will be fine. Somehow all is as it is meant to be.'

Rosemary did not fully understand. 'It's a remarkable...'

'Yes yes. But that is what I do. It has turned out rather better than I hoped.'

Rosemary wanted to hug her.

'You don't look very well, Murielle.'

'For an artist, dying young is not such a disaster. On a personal level, it sucks.'

'I'm so sorry.'

'Don't be. I have made my peace, thanks to Rafael.'

'Will you give me an email address or something? I'll be off tomorrow.'

'A better idea: I'll see you in Santiago. Do you think Rafael would take me in his car? You will have to ask him for me. We'll celebrate together and then, maybe, I will go home.'

The fear is that death will be a night of wolves. Rafael says it will not be and I am not to be afraid. I am to take death by the horns, as I have taken life and live it. I must give, he says, to those who love me more than I love them. There is only love. If there is love in my statues then they will endure. I must think about this. My life, my work, has been filled with scorn for the ridiculousness of other people, for the big joke of life. Now it is over and I am not sure I am laughing.

TWENTY-NINE

Rain flooded the route the day Rosemary left Rafael's. And pilgrims, arriving at a leaking hostel, dispirited and dripping, climbed into their sleeping bags and listened to it fall. Loud and insistent, it drummed on a jumble of plastic bags where the roof had given way. The old pilgrim, whose bags they were, appeared not to notice. Finally, the noise annoyed another so much he climbed out of bed and shook the man with vehemence, pointing to the pool of water on the floor and shouting at him in German. When the old boy eventually got the message he thanked the ruffian profusely before decamping; still thanking long after he got comfortable in a different bunk. Then peace. Rain still fell in a thick mist wrapping round the pilgrims who slept as if spellbound for a thousand years.

When Rosemary opened her eyes a man stood beside her. His face was so close to hers on her top bunk that it was alarming. He kissed her on the mouth and would have kept on kissing her with more dry, out of practice kisses had she not sat up out of reach. This was a new phenomenon; perhaps needing a padlock for the zip of her sleeping bag. He was lonely, he said, a widower from Quebec. His friends had told him that the Camino was a good place to find a new wife. Rosemary struggled for the right phrase, 'Desist!' or, 'Unhand me old timer!' She settled for, 'I am married.'

He looked so sad she nearly apologized. He took out a little pot of tiger balm from his pocket.

'Here you can have this, I don't need this anymore.'

'Thank you very much.'

She wondered if it was just for married people and what help it would be to connubial bliss. The Canadian asked her to eat with him, to show there were no hard feelings. In the only available café on the hairpin bend of a two-lane mountain pass with the tumbledown cluster of the hostel and the café, a pit stop for long distance lorry drivers, the owner sold wine wholesale and also provided meals. After the meal the owner opened the door to a store to fetch grapes for the French Canadian and let out a shriek as a couple of rats ran out fast through her shop and in to the rain. The French Canadian ate the grapes with a shrug and the briefest of inspections.

'She should have shot the rats,' he said.

For Rosemary the days passed as a series of images, glistening with promise, bright as beads. She could not be despondent, however sorry she felt for Murielle. It was tawdry to have envied Murielle's life in Lyon; the freedom she had described of life under the golden dome with a flat of her own. That she had been an artist and not a wife or a mother had seemed to Rosemary so rich, unattainable yet desirable. Now it did not seem such a prize. Perhaps Murielle did not waste time wishing for what could never be.

All the problems of walking that had been insurmountable had evaporated. Rosemary had become so accustomed to her carapace that it was a part of her, as light as a jacket and as easily put on. Without the throb of pain in her ankles she felt fit. Completing the walk was now a distinct possibility; only an inch of the daunting red line on the map remained. She was ready to chart a new life as one who had lived the dream, who had achieved, who had been a contender. Now that it was inevitable she would arrive in Santiago on her own two feet, it was time to enjoy every last step and walk the Spanish way; no introspection; no more tears. Rosemary took the yellow arrow from round her neck; the arrow that only she and Dominic had worn and put it safely in her purse. Goodbye to all that. She made a conscious decision to banish thoughts of the hermetic grey skies of Manchester. Music would be faced in good time and maybe she would dance. Words flooded her head with the rhythm of walking, snatches of poetry, snatches of songs from her past that had lodged in her memory since the day she had heard them. She began to sing, at first softly, then, since she was entirely alone, she tried filling her lungs and sang bel canto.

The following day's climb was steep as stairs in parts and the going was slow. Pilgrims followed close on each other's heels. O Cebreiro, celebrated medieval village still with round houses and thatched roofs, rolled in mist as if they had stumbled into a distant century. The famed view was obscured and the line of pilgrims trundled on through. Eventually it stopped raining and Rosemary hummed opera, *sotto voce*. The ruffian from the night before, a few paces behind, reached forward and put his hand on her shoulder, startling her as if she had been caught doing something illegal.

'But you are English, how come you know opera?'

His shoulders heaved silently, as his own joke consumed him.

Gradually, the gradient became more forgiving and the line of pilgrims stretched out till solitude replaced the loneliness of walking with strangers.

From the top it was down hill into a new land, though sadly, not all the way, according to her book. Galicia: the last province. Gone was the breath taking emptiness of the Meseta and dramatic horizons of Navarra or Rioja scarred by the track disappearing to infinity. Instead, the path wound through gentle, lush fields, bordered by abundant wild flowers, autumn crocus, even gentians. Tiny hamlets of medieval houses with jutting wooden balconies and adobe or stonewalls were as frequent as the showers. It felt like stepping back into another world, another time: farmers, families, hay lofts, *horeos*: those stone boxes on stilts like coffins on legs for storing maize and grain and keeping it free from rats or floods. Eucalyptus forests blotted out huge sections of sky and much of the sunlight, leaving glimpses of jewel blue above and patches of warmth on the ground. Their clinical smell filled the lungs with cold precision. Villagers, sometimes with their herds, would stop and pass the time of day. They spoke a different language and their desire to press well wishes or advice on passing pilgrims met with baffled expressions and apologetic shrugs. Or else they simply did not notice passing pilgrims and managed to look right through them.

There was a girl in a hayloft with raven hair and blue eyes. Her youth and beauty beamed down on pilgrims passing at ground level and could be seen from far off. Perhaps she had been placed there out of harm's way; or perhaps she was a siren, a lure for all young men. A second woman poked her head up beside the beauty; wizened and shrunken, old enough to be her great grandmother twice removed or even to have risen from the grave; a warning to all that beauty fades and life is transient. The old woman threw back her head and cackled, one solitary tooth in the cavern of her mouth prevented falling into the abyss, as if she was endlessly playing a trick on unsuspecting travellers.

179

*

Memories of home and the walk swirled in an eddy and Rosemary was wistful for company. Light barely penetrated a tunnel of trees that swallowed the path. Something lurked ahead, a darting, dark movement, a loud crack of twigs underfoot and the thrash of a large animal hidden in undergrowth: just the place for wild boar. The grip of fear was electrifying: the sudden flurry of the heart did not settle back to its reassuring rhythm. Each step forward became more hesitant, the desire to turn and run almost overwhelming. A glance behind revealed the exit, clear but distant, ahead, a similar distant bright hole. There was no one in sight.

To brave a bear one must pretend to be larger, puff out the chest and step boldly. This was the method adopted to deter the wild boar. Rosemary drew herself to her full five feet and stamped along the path until a flash of metal caught the air, unmistakable in the gloom. A person, with a knife. Rosemary inched forward hoping to pass unnoticed.

As she drew near she could see a man seated in an oasis, a fountain and a resting place beside the path. He was eating, pen knife in hand. On the wall beside him was his picnic wrapped in brightly coloured paper suggesting it was from a specialist shop. She could smell it. He called, *Buen Camino*, in a very non-threatening way. Her reply was automatic, *Qué aproveche,* a phrase she had heard so often in Spain; a wish for the well being of those eating. He offered her some of his picnic, *No, gracias*, again the answer was automatic, still thinking of boars and assassins and that she should escape.

'Rosa Maria.'

Finally she stopped as if coming to earth and turned back.

'*Pero bueno, José Luis, qué susto.*' You really scared me.

He looked puzzled, but an attempt at explaining in Spanish that she had taken him for a wild boar or a knife-wielding murderer did not bear thinking. She laughed with relief and delight at the sight of Jose Luis' friendly face. He pointed expectantly to his pie with his knife and she accepted. His eyes danced as if he was amused.

'It is a speciality of Galicia and very delicious,' he had a way of pronouncing 'N' as if it was always followed by a silent 'G', which she had not noticed before.

José Luis cut a generous slice of his *empañada*, a sort of puff pastry pizza, filled with tuna, tomatoes, peppers and black olives. It was delicious. Rosemary sat beside him, feeling the stone of the wall through her shorts. The world was peaceful and silent, but for the trickle of water from the pipe of the fountain into the stone trough that made the water look black, pure and inviting.

'Don't drink the water in Galicia,' José Luis said as if reading her thoughts.

He was Spanish so he must know.

It was just his advice, she could take it or leave it; he would not be drinking the water, ever.

Was there an explanation?

Ya verás. His final word.

In Galicia there are so many animals; cows, goats, all wandering freely through villages; small herds moved by single farmers or their wives, mothers or daughters from one field to another. It was quite likely that the water table would be polluted; rain and excrement everywhere; a rural idyll.

José Luis had a relaxed way of walking, a relaxed

181

pace of life. Any bar that presented itself as appealing was worth a pit stop, any joke worth laughing at, any local worth passing the time of day with. His attitude was upbeat and pleasing; she adopted the even tenor of his days. At approximately two pm for the next few days they stopped for *menu del dia;* a civilised meal in the middle of the day, which rather than induce sleepiness, which Rosemary had suspected, renewed energy and optimism. The most unpromising bars, knee deep in papers, cocktail sticks and olive stones had a *comedor*, a quiet back room full of tables modestly laid with cloths and flowers. First, José Luis would check the restaurant and if it was full of white collar and manual workers, eating extremely well with no frills, no fuss, just good, peasant food, beautifully served, they would seat themselves at a table where, no sooner seated, a waiter would bring bread and carafes of water and wine or, better and more usually, open new bottles at the table. Three quarters of an hour, perhaps double, eating in comfort, felt luxurious.

'Not luxury,' José Luis would insist, 'just normal.'

Here the peasants ate everything; mussels and prawns; sweet smelling, fresh fish of all descriptions; steak. Even tripe became a delicacy cooked with chickpeas and chorizo.

However, most afternoons José Luis' pace outstripped hers. He would turn and call, wait for her to catch up, offer her a fistful of small boiled sweets, insisting with a bow that she should help herself, *'Caramelos*, Rosa Maria' and gradually would disappear from view. They would meet up at the hostel in the evening.

One such afternoon was pleasantly cool, the path, a quiet byway, stretched before her and her destination,

Casanova, a comfortable distance ahead. Rosemary's mind was empty but for birdsong and the rustle of leaves. She did not notice a pilgrim catch up behind her and was surprised when Ria, even browner than before, called cheerily.

They stopped at a stall selling blackberries that an enterprising old woman had set up beside the path.

'These'll quench your thirst on the long way ahead,' she coaxed. They were both tempted, even though the price was steep. Within five minutes they had arrived at the municipal refuge whose door opened almost directly onto the path and laughed at the woman's marketing ploy. In a simple garden to one side José Luis, discrete and gentlemanly, was writing to his son. When he saw that they both carried blackberries he clicked his tongue, '*Lobo. Que lobos son.*' What wolves some people are! And he was quite put out on their behalf.

The caretaker's small dark eyes flitted over Rosemary and Ria as they entered the hostel. He supervised as they signed themselves in. He escorted them upstairs where he unlocked one of several doors and stood over them as they laid out their bedding. When he seemed reluctant to leave they presented a united front, folded their arms and all but pushed him back through the door, closing it behind him. They congratulated each other on their good fortune; having arrived early enough to have hot water in the shower, having spanking new beds in an airy room and having the dormitory to themselves for the time being. From the vantage of their upstairs window they could see successive small groups of pilgrims as they hesitated at the door and then turned away and carried on walking. No one else signed in the whole afternoon.

In the garden José Luis had a proposition for

183

them. That evening he was going to eat in a restaurant in a nearby village famous for its octopus. Some acquaintances, wealthy businessmen who were travelling the Camino with the benefit of a car and the luxury of hotels, were going to give him a lift. He was sure they would be delighted if Rosemary and Ria joined them.

The women looked at each other and accepted happily. Rosemary had noticed that a large meal in the middle of the day left a hunger of tremendous proportions by nightfall. The unassuming José Luis, pleased at the arrangement, quietly picked up his pen and continued to write. The caretaker could be heard calling, 'Where is the woman who is thirty eight?' They shrugged.

'Where is the woman who is thirty eight?' an imperious, more urgent tone. It was a strange request, but the women assumed that having looked at the log book, where both had dutifully signed in, he had discovered that some important fact had been left out. He looked a jobs-worth, prepared to be punctilious over nothing.

'It must be you,' Rosemary said to Ria with a laugh, 'Shall I come with you?' and they both went to find him.

The caretaker was waiting near the door where the register lay. He completely ignored Rosemary and addressed all comments to Ria. He wanted to know why she was travelling the Camino and if she was alone.

'Yes I am alone and I am walking because I'm a workaholic and I'm trying to break the habit.'

This much Rosemary had heard her tell before and she fiddled with books and trays of blackberries left on a side table in the room. Mentally she justified her presence. She was acting as chaperone, an older

184

woman lending moral support. She was surprised Ria had not told him to mind his own business. Or at least ask why he wanted to know. Perhaps, having told her reasons so many times and having asked herself the same question over and over the answer was automatic. Then Ria spoke again, a sentence spoken aloud that really was an innermost thought, best left unsaid.

'Actually, I don't think my partner still loves me and I want to know what, if anything, I am going to do about it.'

The caretaker's beady eyes lit up and he stepped closer to Ria. Rosemary could not help wanting to hear and she too took a step closer. It seemed as if Ria had seen inside her heart and voiced what was nagging away. She waited, with slight misgiving at her voyeurism, for great and relevant advice to fall from the small man's mouth.

He asked Ria to live with him. It was obviously an opportunity he had been waiting for and a question he was used to popping. He told Ria of his wealth and his prospects and all that could be hers if only she agreed to be his. He produced a card with his details, pressed it into her hand and implored her to get in touch once the situation at home was clear.
It was as if merely living in a village called Casanova, had made him adopt the role of the eponymous anti hero.

Ria looked a little startled by her own revelation. When Casanova asked her for a kiss on account, she looked like someone who has been a long way off for a long time who is suddenly asked to make a life changing decision. Rosemary, in the background, silently urged Ria to make the right decision. Ria refused point blank, and Rosemary uttered aloud, 'Oh thank God' thus successfully reminding

185

Casanova that he was not alone with the future love object. He glared at Rosemary. He promised he would be back later for the little kiss to seal the deal and with the treat of some coffee for the morning. 'Just for you, you understand,' he pointed at Ria.

'My God,' Ria was flustered and a little flushed, 'I don't know why I said that. I usually have a stock answer for such odious types.'

Ria explained that she had spent time away from her partner on a couple of occasions to try to make sense of their relationship.

'Did it work?' Rosemary asked and a sweet expression passed over Ria's face.

'For a while, but like most cures, it is only ever a temporary measure. Why do you think I am here?'

Rosemary felt she had stern questions to answer; not only concerning her own relationship, but the way she made summary decisions that were seldom just or correct about the people she met.

'I am sorry you feel that way, about your partner,' Rosemary said, 'Not a nice feeling and not an easy decision.'

'You see,' Ria continued, 'We can't have children so we have thrown ourselves into our work and sometimes it takes us over. He is a doctor also.'

For a moment there was a sense of enormous sadness in the room. Then a horn tooted as a flashy sports car drew up outside the hostel.

'That might be our lift,' Rosemary said, 'Are you still OK to go?'

Ria nodded.

THIRTY

Rafael drizzled oil on the remains of last night's bread he had toasted for his breakfast and felt too tired to raise it to his mouth. Any moment he was sure Stefan would bound into his kitchen and dog his footsteps for another day. When he prepared a meal Stefan wanted to help; when he sat to read Stefan joined him; when he went to contemplate Murielle's mural Stefan came too. Rafael felt like shaking him and demanding, 'What? What is it that you want?'

Eventually he had told Stefan to walk; that would be the best cure for his ills.

'Walk and keep asking yourself what it is that God wants of you; an answer will come.'

He had given that advice many times, he thought it was sound, but had only once had feedback in the form of a letter from a man thanking him for his kindness.

To Stefan he had spoken wearily as a man from whom too much has been asked too many times. He had no words left. Whether that was because of Murielle or because of Stefan or even Dominic, he could not tell. It was unusual for any pilgrim to spend more than a couple of nights in one place. He tried to guard against ugly thoughts that sometimes crowded, but he couldn't be sure they hadn't taken advantage of his hospitality. He tried to stay above the tedium and yet that is how he spent his days; accepting humbly those very everyday tasks in order to physically care for these souls. How did they repay him? They behaved no better than beasts in the field. No, he did not, would not, think that.

This was his last morning. The last time he would put on music to awaken his pilgrims and the last time he would urge them towards a spiritual life; the last time he would encourage them to keep walking. The whole point of the pilgrimage was to keep walking; that is what he believed. No matter how weary, whether from the world or from walking, it was best each morning to rise with the sun and set off.

Once he had seen off the last of the cyclists with their raucous voices and Stefan, of course, he would prepare to shut the refuge. If no one came to open it, then pilgrims would have to shift for themselves: walk on to the next village or simply sleep in the garden. Theoretically, there was nothing to stop them doing this. His replacement had not arrived as arranged. Even with two days' grace he had simply not turned up.

Rafael inhaled deeply, breathing in the perfume of incense sticks that Murielle had lit that morning as she had every morning since she had been there. He had a duty to Murielle; she needed to go home and he had to help her. He shook his head to collect his thoughts and went to load suitcases into his car.

For Stefan rebuffs were part of life: in the orphanage he was used to having requests denied. Once, he had asked a care worker to advertise for parents for him; someone, anyone, even if he could only be adopted part time. He had never had an answer. He had never given up hope, although the advertisement was never mentioned again. The day he left the home for good he questioned the same care worker to see if he remembered.

'Stefan, you were so young. How could I break it to you? There was only one reply, from a woman who offered to take you for tea once a month.'

Stefan explained that was all he had hoped for; just a small gesture to make life bearable. He could think about it now, of course, without it being unbearable.

He had to find Murielle to say goodbye, but he couldn't find her and consoled himself with the thought that he might meet up with Dominic.

'Sod walking,' he said aloud. To reach Santiago by foot would take at least a week; by bus, he could be there in a matter of hours.

The bus dropped Stefan on the outskirts of Santiago, in the workaday bustle of a busy city. A short walk took him through the tracery of medieval streets to the Cathedral Square. He climbed immense steps outside the cathedral and pushed his way in, past beggars and tourist and pilgrims milling at the door. Mass was about to start and a choir was singing rather well. They belonged to a church group from Germany, according to a rumour that ran the length of the benches, who paid to have the *botefumeiro* swung. The huge incense burner took eight men to swing and he had a fine view. He took it as a good omen. The congregation was restless with tourists and pilgrims arriving, fit and weathered and jubilant. The nave and the aisles in front, behind and to either side were a sea of shifting heads and faces. They did not interest Stefan. He let his eyes scan the rows as the smell of incense and the soaring voices filled his consciousness. Dominic was not hard to identify. Even at a distance of nearly a hundred feet his blond head stood out above the rest.

Suffocated by the mumbo jumbo, Stefan pushed his way out of the cathedral and ambled round to the far side where he had seen Dominic. He chose a prominent, sunny table of a bar that was playing Galician music with a view of the cathedral side door. He ordered a beer and took a long swig; the

189

secular music, floating flutes and folk tunes, the sun and the beer suited his mood much better. His phone vibrated in his pocket; he had actually forgotten it was there. He breathed deeply and laid the phone in front of him on the table; he would at least see who it was from.

Pilgrims began to spill out across the square to the side of the Cathedral; the sound of their laughter punctuated the music. Finally, there was Dominic, tall in the sunshine, dressed in black. When he walked into a patch of shade he completely disappeared and took so long to walk back into a patch of sun that Stefan began to doubt he had seen him.

Dominic did not notice Stefan till the last moment. Stefan was gratified by the look of pleasure on his face; the Flying Dutchman had not forgotten him. It is easy to forget some people on the Camino, perhaps due to the physical exertion of walking, the shifting scenery or the daily routine that tends to monotony. Faces and days collided and receded in a jumble; a phenomenon Stefan had noted with interest. Perhaps that is why nearly everyone kept a journal: just to remember what day it was. Other faces were unforgettable. Dominic's hair was cropped short and Stefan presumed he had prevailed on another woman to cut it for him, remembering with discomfort the intimate scene with Rosemary. Why couldn't he go to a barber's like a normal person?

'Stefan,' Dominic's voice was reassuring.

'The Flying Dutchman, no less; thought I might catch up with you.'

There were smiles and exclamations of how well each looked and anecdotes to share. Dominic sat with him at the table and smiled at Stefan,

'You're looking good.'

'See you've recently had a new haircut.' Stefan

eyed him sternly and something in the puritan tone
infuriated the Dutchman. He was no longer willing
to put up with disapprobation from this younger
man; a man who didn't know up from down when it
came to relationships and deliberately turned love
into a sick psychodrama. Dominic was taken aback
by his uncharacteristic lack of charity and loss of
self-control. He reined himself in, worked his jaw
muscles till the waiter arrived.

'Want another?' Stefan nodded, 'Two beers,
please.'

Before Dominic finished rolling his cigarette, a
slow deliberate act that enabled him to keep his eyes
away from Stefan, he decided to make a light of it.

'There was one woman, tall, French and blonde,
the best fuck of the whole Camino.'

'Not, Murielle?'

'Don't tell me you scored too.'

Stefan lunged at him, aiming to grab him by the
ears, a prominent feature now his hair was short. He
missed when Dominic dodged and succeeding in
knocking over both bottles of beer when he landed
heavily on the table. The amber liquid splashed on to
the stones and up Dominic's bare legs. Dominic let
out one word of surprise, 'Wo' and reached
instinctively to rescue the bottles and what remained
of the beer.

'She's a sick woman, you animal,' Stefan growled;
he truly hated Dominic at this moment.

'I was only joking about the best fuck. She wanted
consoling and I happened to be there.'

Beer had soaked Dominic's cigarette and he rolled
another rapidly from his tin, scooting off beer from
the lid. He inhaled deeply feeling the smoke calm his
nerves.

'So,' he ventured, as if testing water he expected

would be volatile.

'It really pisses me off the way you use people. You leave a trail of destruction, you do know that?'

Stefan summoned the waiter for replacement beers and asked to have the table cleaned and then watched him as he deftly swept the cloth as if to wipe the slate. The pause allowed breath to steady and Stefan started over.

'I have some news.'

He did not take his eyes from the waiter who, still balancing his tray with one hand, replaced the cloth and opened the bottles at the table, lingering longer than necessary in case he might need to prevent a scuffle.

'My film.'

Dominic braced himself for the worst.

Stefan continued, 'It did OK.' He could not prevent the smile twitching at his lips. However much he tried to conceal his glee, he felt his heart tremor with excitement. Yes, yes, oh yes. He accepted his rightful place as it settled quietly round him. The film world, his chosen world, had recognised him as one of their own. Not a golden bear, not even silver: he had not competed for one of those: the film was too experimental, just praise was enough.

Dominic raised his beer in salute then, putting his bottle down as if he'd changed his mind, took hold of Stefan's hand in both his and shook it warmly. He looked as if he might shed tears and was far more emotional than Stefan.

'You know that's the best news ever.'

They chinked bottles. Dominic drank deeply, appreciating the cold bubbles on the back of his throat where it had gone dry,

'Have you told Inge yet?'

'I don't think she needs to know. I'm telling *you*.'

Dominic smiled, his cool nearly restored,

'I'm walking on to Finisterra tonight. Why don't you come? There's a young couple going too, you'd like them. She's Dutch and he's English, just left the priesthood.'

Stefan laughed, 'Sounds an interesting mix. Why exactly are you walking through the night?'

'Well, there's my reputation to live up to.'

'You already have your nickname.'

'Seriously, I don't have much time. I want to do it and I want to be back here with a day in hand. There's a few people I want to say goodbye to who haven't got to Santiago yet.'

Stefan nodded. 'Rosemary, you mean?'

'No, I think we said our goodbyes. Have you seen her?'

Stefan said he had seen her several times and had liked her more. She had been good for him. Then he asked Dominic's permission to roll himself a cigarette.

'Help yourself.' Dominic implied there was no need to ask.

When he had licked the glue and had taken the first satisfying breath of smoke Stefan tackled Dominic, 'You didn't treat her very well. You want to watch out or you'll get yourself a bad name.'

Although Dominic laughed he was uncomfortable.

'You better come with me to Finisterra and keep me in check.'

'Thanks for the offer, but I've unfinished business too. I want to tell Rosemary my good news. I'll take a bus back and catch up with her. I only heard just now, and apart from you I'd like to tell her. She—that is—we…'

Dominic laughed and it was on the tip of his

tongue to call Stefan a rogue.

'It's not what you think,' Stefan said defensively, seeing the expression on his face, 'She's helped me a lot to get over Inge.'

Stefan reached for his top pocket and took out his light meter, small and solid in his hand.

'And I'm flying back to Germany in a couple of days. I've got an idea for my next film. I'm looking for backers if you're interested. Thought I'd call it, *The Camino Show.*

Their laughter rang out, a good honest sound.

THIRTY-ONE

José Luis was waiting for Ria and Rosemary with the car door open. He ushered them into the back seat with a small a bow and climbed in beside them. The driver, Raul, greeted them without turning round. He eyed them in the rear view mirror and was already revving the engine. His companion, Martín, turned his head long enough to show his gold teeth. They both wore huge linked gold bracelets and signet rings like knuckle dusters, more like gangsters than business men. Raul drove as if this was a getaway car after a heist. They narrowly missed colliding with a fast moving car as they emerged onto a main road, with a screech and a smell of burning rubber. Rosemary and Ria exchanged glances. Ria held the swinging handle tightly and Rosemary, sandwiched between Ria and José Luis slid helplessly across the leather seat between them.

José Luis remonstrated about the driving, but Raul and Martín laughed off his concerns. Neither Rosemary nor Ria could keep up with the quick fire Spanish. They refused to believe that José Luis had much in common with Raul and Martín, although both found it all too plausible that Raul did not have a driving license. Their glance, one to the other, was a quiet prayer that they would arrive in one piece.

The restaurant was not unlike an old Chinese laundry with a rush job on. Huge cauldrons bubbled, producing vast clouds of steam. Octopus heads bobbed in fast boiling red wine, tentacles wafting aimlessly. The *patrona* was keen for everyone to take a look. She demonstrated as she moved between the vats with sleeves rolled and a pair of wooden tongs, like those used to fish washing out of a twin tub in the sixties and seventies. She used these to grasp each octopus in turn, raise it high till its legs dangled clear of the liquid, dunk it three times before letting it submerge with a little plop and leaving it to cook for a few more minutes, while she moved on to the next vat and the next. Then one by one each bedraggled octopus was cut up swiftly with sharp scissors. Purple discs with suckers fell in a mound on waiting wooden platters. They were sprinkled with paprika and drizzled in olive oil before being presented to a waiting table. The suckers looked alien; but the taste was good and not in the least rubbery.

Pilgrims squashed along tables, more platters of *pulpo* were ordered, more wine, more bread, more laughter and the night was festive.

Then there were voices of dissent. Not an argument. A group of Spaniards started to grumble about their sleeping quarters and close questioned one of the business men about where he was staying. He looked remarkably shifty, as if by confessing to a comfortable hotel room in a town nearby he would be turned out of the restaurant on his ear or, at the least, lose all credence as a pilgrim. He looked to José Luis for assistance. José Luis exaggerated the comforts of Casanova; the luxury of staying in an empty hostel with a choice of beds. When he said, indicating Rosemary and Ria, that they were all staying there, the Spaniards were incredulous.

'That sly son of a whore; that filthy lying pig; he is not to be trusted.'

José Luis encouraged them to get on with their story without the expletives, with anxious glances in the direction of his female companions, worried that they would take offence.

It seemed Casanova had denied them all access, saying that there was absolutely no room.

'He could see I was limping; look at my bandage.'

All eyes turned and looked at the outsize foot swathed in bandages.

'I told him I was sure it was broken; stress fracture from too much walking; a spontaneous break. Imagine how painful. He turned us away at the door. I didn't believe it was full; there was no noise and only you in the garden.'

He looked accusingly at José Luis.

There were commiserations that the young men had to walk the extra ten kilometres. There were explanations sought, hypotheses put forward, till the topic was exhausted.

Ria was exhausted too. All the noise, the wine and excitement was too much. She begged to be taken back to the hostel. She apologised for breaking up the party, but secretly even the businessmen were grateful to make their excuses. A long discussion followed about who should pay for what; how many platters of *pulpo* they owed for and who had been in which group. So many people had joined the tables and things threatened to become heated and then just as easily were good naturedly settled. Everyone paid five euros and that was that.

As they were leaving, Stefan walked through the door. He wanted Rosemary to stay; the businessmen were pressing her to go; she was apologetic. The flashy car was outside, engine running. Noise from the restaurant flowed into the street. They stood in the doorway and Stefan took out his light meter and gave it to Rosemary.

'A keepsake.'

'You can't give this away.'

He smiled, 'I've got a spare.' He pulled a card from his pocket and gave that to her too. 'Look me up, sometime.'

In the car on the journey back to the hostel Ria was terrified as the vehicle careered along narrow lanes in the dark. Again Rosemary slid helplessly, first one way then the other between Ria and José Luis on the back seat.

True to his word, Casanova had brought the coffee for the morning, as he said he would. He was still waiting for Ria to claim his kiss. The chase round the table and chairs, Casanova pursuing first one woman and then the other, ended only when José Luis commanded him to stop and in rich tones told him he should be ashamed of himself. Casanova beat a hasty retreat. José Luis was pink and apoplectic that they—and by this time both were breathless and incapacitated with laughter—should have been subjected to such behaviour by a Spaniard purporting to be a *hospitalero.*

'*Pero bueno, homre!*'

Rosemary made her way to the bedroom and found she still had her fists clenched round Stefan's gifts. Somehow she knew that the unsatisfactory meeting in the doorway of the *pulpo* restaurant would be the last she would see of him. She had the feeling that she had let him down. She smoothed the card, which held four words: Stefan Tarazin, Film Maker. She squinted through the prism but, to her eyes, the world did not look any different.

The following day Rosemary, Ria and José Luis walked together till nightfall, arriving at a hostel where pilgrims who had partied into the night at the *pulpo* restaurant were already preparing to sleep. They grumbled and sighed at the noise the latecomers made, giving the hostel the air of an old people's

198

home. The three amigos tiptoed about too excited to rest. The prospect of arriving in Santiago the following day created an enormous energy that only partying into the small hours could lessen. Since they had missed the party the night before and their desire to be full of laughter would disturb the slumberers, they took a taxi to the next village and found a restaurant; a surprise to find such a clean and well-maintained establishment in so small a village. It had a large blackboard outside the door listing fish and fish dishes that were fresh that day.

José Luis found a table for them and then greeted several of the other diners, as long lost friends, only some of whom were pilgrims. It was another joyous occasion of the type that epitomised Spanish life where optimism was irrepressible. Joi de vivre erupted in laughter and lingered in cigarette smoke and the aroma of fresh roasted garlic in the pleasant dining room.

José Luis asked the *patrona* what she would recommend from her large menu. In fact there did not seem anything that was not of the freshest and not worth trying. Other diners were called on to comment how their meal was. Were they enjoying their such and such? Wasn't the such and such to die for? The *patrona* recommended clams in wine sauce as a house speciality and when Rosemary confessed to never having eaten clams in her life, insisted that they accept a large dish for free. Another table of pilgrims had a bottle of wine sent over, raising their own glasses in cheers and recognition of the fact that they too would soon be arriving in Santiago.

'Do you know them?' Ria asked.

'Never seen them before.' José Luis did not marvel at the generosity; he considered it a normal courtesy and invited the fellow pilgrims to join their table and share the wine. An evening that would have been merely enjoyable improved and became a party. Rosemary and Ria were prepared to be overwhelmed. They felt as children might when allowed to stay up late for the first time and sample the delights of a grown up world. They could not understand all the jokes, but laughed with everyone else for the sheer joy of laughing. In their native lands this life of ease was reserved, like an exclusive club, for the decidedly well off.

That night sleep was easy. Ria was quickly asleep. Rosemary thought she would lie awake thinking of home, but she too slept dreamlessly the instant she closed her eyes.

The next morning, triumphant and smiling, unable to believe they had walked so fast and so far, they arrived in Santiago in time to queue in the office that issued the prized *compostella;* a beautiful certificate proved they were *bone fide* pilgrims after walking the Camino. Rosemary laughed when she heard the question asked repeatedly, 'Why did you walk the Camino? For sport or for spiritual reasons?' She heard José Luis admit to spiritual. Ria claimed she had walked for sport.

They could hear all the bells of Santiago ringing, each church setting off their peal of bells one after another till the sound calling the faithful, tourists and pilgrims to church, a clarion call, could no longer be ignored. They were in time for Mass in the cathedral at noon, hurrying across the beautiful square, barely looking left or right, weaving deftly between groups planted firmly in the way like rocks that would happily wreck their advance. Inside, rucksacks were piled high round pillars like sandbags expecting a disaster or shoring up a crumbling edifice.

José Luis pushed his way into an already full bench with no sign of his usual perfect manners. He did not turn to bid them farewell or check to see if they found somewhere to sit. He kept his grey head resolutely forward and concentrated on the spectacle; a loving but stern parent, finally free of his charges. José Luis remained a private man. He did not wallow in problems, either his or others'. Life was an entirely different matter: that was for living and sharing. Rosemary knew he had been teaching her how to live. She had been in pieces and he had shown her how to reassemble. He had encouraged and expected her to walk on her own feet. She tried to measure up like a dutiful daughter.

Several priests were on the altar and eight men came to swing the incense burner, so huge and heavy it was suspended from the roof by chains. It took all eight to hoist and swing it, sending it high over the congregation's heads from one end of the nave towards the other. The momentum swept them off their feet. It was easy, then, to see where Buñuel sourced his religious imagery. The idea had been to disinfect rather than bless the great swathes of pilgrims sitting in the pews. Now it was a spectacle that had to be requested and paid for .

The sound of a mobile phone nearby interrupted the show. Ria whispered to Rosemary that her partner had sent her a text to say that he was flying in that afternoon and had booked a hotel room for them. Ria was all smiles and hugged Rosemary.

'I hope things work out for you, too.'

'Thanks. I'm really pleased for you.'

'He is taking me to a restaurant tonight to celebrate, otherwise I would have loved to eat with you.'

'Don't even think of it.'

With a sense of guilt Rosemary listened to the service and the sweet voices of a choir. She was relieved Seb was not arriving to celebrate with her. She knew he would have loved to come, but would not unless she asked him. She was not ready to see him, nor yet to go straight home. She made a decision then to walk for three more days and take time to reflect on the journey before flying back to her family.

A rumour ran round the cathedral as Mass ended. People she knew, people she hardly knew, as they hugged each other in congratulations, had a message for Rosemary.

'Dominic is looking for you.' or, 'the Flying Dutchman is outside. He will wait for you in the square, after Mass.'

Rosemary's breath caught in surprise. Ria smiled,

'There you see. That is some Camino good fortune that you should meet up again.'

THIRTY-TWO

Dominic sat in the square. He took out his notebook and pencil but his mind wandered. He was weary. Blood throbbed at his temples and in his ears, an adrenaline rush as if he was about to perform. Something was urging him to complete his odyssey like the instinct that would compel a bird to fly over perilous seas to return to a waiting mate. He imagined an outsize bird with a vast wingspan, perhaps an albatross, whose capacity for love and nurture often cost their life, preferring to die rather than abandon their young.

He thought of the statue he and his young companions had seen looming in the early morning on their way to the coast. A family scene: a giant of a man striding out, with his wife and little ones clinging to his coat tails as if begging him not to go. The man's head was held high, his gaze to the horizon, not seeing the look of desperation on those he wanted to leave behind. Dominic knew that feeling: a man must do what a man must do, however hard, and leave family and responsibilities behind. Now he wanted to be home but there was unfinished business.

He hated waiting but he had made a promise that he would, to himself and to Stefan, who had succeeded in making him feel guilty. His words had troubled him all the way to Finisterra and back. *The way you use people really pisses me off.* Stefan had been so angry. And maybe he did owe it to Rosemary to see her again. He was not used to criticism. He hated anyone to think badly of him and he certainly did not want to think badly of himself.

He had walked through the night to get back to

Santiago in order to spread the word that he was looking for Rosemary. The bus would have arrived too late and if he missed her in the cathedral then it would be harder and harder to find her. He had led the young couple he was with through the night too, filled with the enthusiasm of their youth. They had survived unscathed, perhaps because they were young and newly in love. He was exhausted. He used to hear his father say he was 'bone tired', the antithesis to 'bone idle', maybe. Now he knew how that felt. The couple had stayed in Finisterra; they made no plans, living day to day. Watching the sunset at the end of the world, night after night, was a splendid thing. He pictured the magenta and turquoise of the sky as he had burned his old clothes there, hoping to rise from the ashes, phoenix like, a new man.

On his way to the rendezvous with Rosemary he had posted his last love letter to Jenneka, his last letter of the Camino that included some suggestions for his homecoming. The words had not flowed as they normally did. The letter had felt stilted and guarded; a lot can happen in a month apart and there were always secrets he would rather not share. It was the same when Jenneka went away. They allowed each other freedom, but they trusted each other to stay true and it had worked well. He usually wrote his love letters with a sense of urgency; letters he hoped would form the basis of a book when he got home. He had a lot riding on this book. His daughter and his son would both be at university and money would be tighter. He was not new to poverty but, so far, he and Jenneka had known nothing like the poverty of his youth; they had merely been hard up; happy, but hard up.

Where is the ease with which I normally write? Words

rapidly filling the page: gone. Replaced by what? The desire to be at home with Janneka and the children. Janneka says they are all fine and I believe her; I am fine too, but we will all be a far sight better when I am home.

And there she is, a little like a scarecrow now. Thin. How did I ever think she was pretty? Maybe I will walk with her and feel again that rhythm and the speed, enjoy the sweat dripping from my face; hold her hand in mine. She has not seen me, but she will. She will run to me like a young lover who has been longing for her man. No, she will walk, sedate and English. Maybe she will no longer find me attractive.

Dominic closed the small notepad and put it in the pocket of his trousers. He must look like a scarecrow himself, dressed as if in someone else's flapping clothes so dusty from the weeks on the road. And his hair—it had taken a punishing. He would go to the barbers before flying home.

The square was jubilant. Sun bounced off three magnificent sides formed by the cathedral and two palaces that had belonged to the kings of Spain, one perhaps built as a magnificent hospice. Rosemary could not be sure and again it did not seem to matter. She scanned the fourth, shaded side of the square and there was Dominic, easy to find, sitting on a low wall. He had nothing with him; he neither read nor wrote; he simply waited. As she walked slowly with the heat bouncing off the flagstones she felt light headed. She imagined running up in slow motion with her arms wide preparing to throw herself into his arms. As she drew closer and he was watching she felt self-conscious. Her clothes, now too big, hampered her progress and seemed to drag her limbs in a tangle, as if they refused to cooperate. She stood beside him; they were the same height when he was sitting down like an adult and a child.

She kissed him lightly on the cheek, a gentle butterfly brush.

'This is a nice surprise.'

But behind her words she thought of Jeeves' long suffering, *'You rang, my lord.'* And there was a temptation to laugh. She recognised the presumption that she would come as bid.

Dominic smiled at how well he had predicted her arrival at this meeting.

'Your bruise has gone,' he said and he lightly touched her cheek. Then, almost disappointed, he said, 'You are not wearing your yellow arrow.'

She put her hand to her throat where it had been. Dominic's arrow still hung round his neck on the clear plastic string.

'You have forgotten me already.'

Still she made no answer, remembering how foolish she had felt one morning seeing the arrow round her neck. She had not thrown it away and she knew she would always keep it. She looked into his face to see how much he was teasing and was undecided. She sat beside him on the wall. Behind them was a drop of several feet onto a straight narrow road that led steeply down hill and out of sight. Wind funnelled onto their backs and Rosemary felt the cold stone of the wall dig into her legs and she shivered.

'What will you do now that you are brown and lovely and strong after the Camino? Will you go home?'

'You might be brown and lovely and strong, Dominic. I don't think anything will have changed for me. I've decided to walk to Finisterra,' she told him as if saying it out loud made it definite.

Dominic said he was glad she had chosen to walk
206

on, 'That's a truly beautiful walk. There is this statue.'

She half listened to his description of the family begging the father not to go. She was aware of his mouth moving, of his hair cut short by a more expert hand, of his black trousers flapping round his spindly legs as if he had borrowed them from a much fatter person. Aware too of his height and the night he had kissed her and she had refused.

'It is hard for women to leave their family too,' she hazarded.

'Yes, but for a man.'

She had known that about him, that he was quite traditional. Perhaps she simply did not know him well enough. That is one advantage twenty-six years of marriage gives. You grow intertwined, perhaps inseparably, but you do know each other.

They told inconsequential details of what had happened since they last met; stilted tales that had seemed funny or meaningful. Then Rosemary said she had seen Stefan a couple of nights back.

'So, you've heard Stefan's good news.'

'What good news?' she asked.

'When I saw him he was full of it and he said he going to look for you to share it with you too.'

'We hardly had time to speak, he just gave me his prism, that little thing he used to look through.'

Dominic was surprised. 'An honour.' He looked at Rosemary as if he was reassessing her.

'He'd heard that the film he was so worried about hadn't panned after all; in fact, it had done quite well.'

'That's great, isn't it? That's a really happy ending.' Rosemary took out the card she had been given and showed it to Dominic. 'He said to look him up sometime. I guess I could Google him.'

Dominic stood up; he was getting chilly. The cold of the stone had seeped to Rosemary's bones.

'Have you kissed the statue yet?'

Rosemary did not know what he meant.

'It's part of the ritual.'

She looked blankly at him and Dominic laughed mirthlessly,

'You really didn't read anything about the Camino before you came.'

He went with her back into the cathedral and waited good naturedly while she queued with a throng of others waiting to kiss and touch statues while being photographed. He sat on the pedestal of a vast pillar with the circumference of a several hundred year old oak tree and borrowed her camera to capture the moment.

'Your family will want to see this.'

'I bet they won't. Still, let's do it.'

In spite of her misgiving, she hoped they would. That was for the future, days away. She willed herself to fall back in to the easy rhythm she and Dominic had shared when they walked together and was aware that too much had happened since. She had tasted the joy of life without introspection, a joy that bubbles up freely from the ground, if you let it.

When she was finished they stepped outside where the sun was blistering after the gloom of the cathedral. The square was quieter with only a few groups of pilgrims still congratulating each other.

'I'll walk with you to leave your rucksack at the hostel. It's some way out of town. An old monastery so huge I don't think it is ever full; best not to risk it though.'

'Are you staying there?' She asked.

Dominic had booked into a hotel, now his pilgrim days were over. He eulogised clean sheets and a private bathroom. There were even weighing scales.

'I have lost ten pounds.' He showed her his gaping

waistband. 'All that clean living on the Camino.'

She smiled and let him run on.

The vast seminary, now used only for pilgrims, sat high on the hill on the edge of Santiago. From outside, the building was splendid with a flight of stone steps. Inside, a vast marble-lined entrance bustled like an airport waiting lounge. She was issued with a set of rules mostly to do with locked doors and the safety of possessions. She left her rucksack with a young volunteer at the desk and was given the number 1,044 as her bed for the night and could easily believe that the building housed so many. Dominic had waited for her on the steps. He had stretched his legs out in front of him and leaned his head back, almost lying and almost asleep.

'I'm not asleep,' he said when she returned, 'but I am suddenly very tired. I walked all night to get here in time to meet you.'

Rosemary wondered why he had not got the bus, but that seemed too practical a suggestion after such a romantic gesture. Instead she said, 'I'm very hungry; I could walk you back to your hotel and then find something to eat.'

'I'm hungry too so after we eat then I'll go for a sleep. I have arranged to meet up with a group of pilgrims tonight in one of the bars. You're welcome to come. We'll probably get a meal then.'

He took her hand and walked back down the hill. They stopped at the main road bristling with people and cars that bordered the modern city and the old. They hurried across and stepped back into the medieval streets.

It was past the time when any restaurant would offer a meal. The best they could hope for was a snack and they were both tetchy by the time they settled on a tiny place tucked away down a side street. The array of *tapas* was bewildering; Rosemary recommended *pulpo* and had to convince Dominic, but here the octopus was rubbery and vinegary and barely edible. Tiredness and a disappointing meal subdued them. Before Dominic set off in one direction and Rosemary in another he stopped to get a map for her from one of many stands.

'Easy to get lost,' he said.

She watched him saunter off, an unrecognisable pace for the Flying Dutchman. He had kept a thread of her like loose cotton and with each step he took she felt herself unravel. Bleak and naked she was completely alone and at a loss. There was not even her carapace to keep her company or to keep her warm and she felt the wind on her back without its protective layer. In the end she walked into the palatial *parador* passing delicately perfumed guests with their soft swish of silk. No one challenged her right to be there, although those who did not look straight through her may have looked askance.

When she reached the sanctuary of the lavatory she was startled by a stranger before she realised who it was. Not a vagrant, not a poor immigrant lavatory cleaner, but her reflection glimpsed in the full-length mirror. The walk had stripped spare flesh from her bones. She felt fit; she looked half starved. She was dumbfounded and sat quite some moments in the spacious cubical of the lavatory till she felt brave enough to face her reflection. She set about reparation and, almost as a ritual, she washed and smoothed her thin limbs with the perfumed lotions provided. There was nothing she could do with hair bleached white. It reminded her of the untidy storks' nests from the beginning of the walk. The birds had no doubt flown in search of better times.

Slightly restored she intended to sit in the hotel lounge till it was time, but courage failed her. Even in normal circumstances the disparity between the guests' grooming and hers would have been intimidating. The urge to lie down was huge. How she would have appreciated the ironed sheets Dominic boasted about. A wall out of sight and out of the wind was the best she could hope for before the afternoon shift started and those wise Spaniards, fed and rested, would start again like starlings enjoying the evening sortie.

There was no such wall; the long trudge to the hostel was the only alternative. By the time she had retrieved her rucksack and found bed number 1,044 it was almost time to leave. She lay on her back in the darkened room aware of how much her clothes gaped. The dormitory was like a vast Nightingale ward from the Crimea. There were no sick or injured or ministering angels, only God-forsaken refugees from life fetched up at these cheap lodgings with a profusion of belongings squalid beside their beds. These were not recognisable pilgrims, just unfortunates come to take advantage of three days' free meals still offered by the *parador*. She was no better than anyone here; prospects were bleak. The solution would be to go home and yet she could not go back home this way. The next day or the next, she would start walking.

She rifled her rucksack but there was nothing to change into so she kept on the baggy shorts and fraying shirt she had worn all day and put on her only jumper over the top. At least her face was clean and her limbs sweet smelling.

THIRTY-THREE

She was first to arrive at the meeting place: the wall in the shaded part of the square where she had met Dominic was still exposed to a chill wind blowing in from the west. She put her back to the wall and waited. The familiar solitude she had come to enjoy began to weigh heavy. She let her mind wander along the Camino and remembered all the tears. She could have cried for England and won first prize. She was tempted to laugh like a mad person.

'Rosemary?' She jumped so much she nearly fell off the wall onto the narrow road below.

Murielle and Rafael stood before her, oddly out of place like parents at a degree-day ceremony. Rafael held Murielle's elbow gently, proprietarily, their bodies curved together like a long-married couple.

'I hoped we would find you,' Murielle said, 'Your phone does not seem to work.'

Rosemary had forgotten they had an arrangement. She stood up and went to embrace them in turn. Murielle's shoulders felt frail. When she went to embrace Rafael she changed her mind and held out her hand, which he shook with warmth and, if she wasn't mistaken, relief that she had not attempted the intimacy of an embrace.

'We are going to eat in the *parador* and hoped you would join us,' Murielle said.

A snug scene in a candlelit room hovered between them, and Rosemary would have claimed a prior engagement even if she had not made one.

'I would love to, but I've arranged to meet a pilgrim I met along the way, Dominic. I think he stayed with you Rafael.'

Rafael's face appeared to close in.

'So many come, so many go.'

He explained that he wanted to take Murielle to eat with the pilgrims behind the kitchen of the *parador*, just for the experience. They were about to turn away. Rafael drew Murielle even closer so they could move as one like a couple in a dance wishing to avoid a collision.

'I could come with you for a while, though.'

Murielle's face brightened.

'Good. That has turned out well.'

Under a wide coach arch at the back entrance to the parador they were met by a concierge, who checked their credentials. Rafael had none but when he said who he was the concierge shook his hand and invited them into his office. Murielle was asked, but shook her head preferring to stand in the queue with the rest. Half a dozen or so waited altogether. Rosemary recognised one young man from the hostel. He was agitated and continually scratched his scalp under his dreadlocks. He had a sandy coloured dog with him on a lead made of an inordinate number of brightly coloured knotted hankies. The concierge was apologetic, but the dog could not come in to the *parador*.

'Can he stay out here then, can he? He can't he? Stay here?' The question rumbled round like thunder in the hills. The look of pleading in the young man's eyes mirrored that of his dog. Murielle asked what the problem was and for a while it looked as if the concierge would refuse. Rafael intervened, turning to the concierge, 'Do you have a bowl? Anything for the dog to drink out of?'

Something in the gentleness of his tone or the simplicity of the solution, helped the concierge to

213

decide in the young man's favour.

'Sure. The dog can tie up to the drainpipe. I'm probably not supposed to, but the kitchen will let you have something for him if you ask.'

The young man smiled and produced bowls, bottled water and a bag of food from the depths of his long coat.

'The dog never goes without.' His smile revealed he cared better for his dog's teeth than for his own.

They were led across an inner courtyard through narrow corridors and up winding stairs past the hotel kitchens to a small dining room where tables were pleasantly laid with tablecloths.

'The staff will be pleased to serve you at the kitchen,' and they were left to their good fortune.

The young man with the dog was chatty. Rosemary was called on to translate first French, then Spanish, then English (for the benefit of a young German couple who had been so kind to her one dark night, who also had shared their stories on the night of the *queimada*) in a dizzying round that she enjoyed.

Murielle ate little. Rafael tried to coax her, but she silenced him with a look and he shrugged. She offered her food to Rosemary.

'It is a pity to waste it. I haven't touched it.'

Rosemary shook her head. She was torn, but it was time to go, she was already late. She was sorry that she did not eat with them, sorry too to have her arrangements topsy-turvy. They agreed to meet again for breakfast there in the pilgrims' dining room. They could say farewell properly. Rafael was going to drive Murielle to the coast and Rosemary would set off walking.

214

It was already dusk and street lamps were lit. It was well past the time they had agreed to meet and the place was empty. Looking about she spotted Dominic at a pavement café nearby and joined him. He looked clean and cared for. He was wearing an eau de nil sweatshirt that suited him perfectly and she imagined that Janneka had chosen it for him. He was surrounded by young people. The Flying Dutchman had made many friends; young men as well as young women had found in him a quality worth following. Their eager faces looked up at him and she felt old. They welcomed her with smiles and made room for her to sit down. There was discussion about where they should eat. In the end a tall young girl took charge; Rosemary did not even know her name.

'Follow me, I know a good place,' she said with an East Coast American accent.

The young American and Dominic led the way and everyone followed as if on a guided tour. The girl was pretty and confident. She too had thought ahead to bring a change of clothes. Her rather glamorous long frock and Dominic's jumper contrasted with the shabbiness of the rest. After the troupe took one or two detours in the confusing alleyways, Rosemary began to think the lead couple were more like generous benefactors taking the mentally insane for an outing.

When they finally arrived the restaurant was almost back where they had started and was pretentious. Rosemary had learned how to judge a good restaurant under José Luis' tutelage. The meal was expensive and insubstantial. And, because they had to be seated outside due to the size of the group, the meal was cold too. Rosemary sat on the edge of the group, near enough to Dominic to see how Miss America batted her eyes.

215

Afterwards they all went to a bar and began to warm up. It was an Irish bar. The beer came in pint glasses and was not light and frothy like Spanish beer. Neither did it have a pleasant effect. The first few mouthfuls sank Rosemary's flagging spirits lower. The bar was dark and crowded and too noisy to talk. She tugged on the sleeve of one of the pilgrims sitting next to her on a bar stool, a young man no older than her son, and offered him the rest of her pint. He accepted with a smile.

Rosemary slipped out into the cool night, uncertain what to do except make her way to the hostel. At night the lovely tangle of medieval streets became a maze. The more she wandered the more confused she became till, too weary to put one foot in front of the other, she sank into the shadows of a shop doorway from sheer weariness like one of the homeless, *una desamparada,* curled up with her head on her knees.

She woke when her shoulder was shaken quite gently.

'Rosa Maria?'

It was the businessmen squatting in front of her. Their gold glinted in the streetlights.

'We thought it was you,' one said.

'But we weren't certain,' said the other.

She wondered if she was dreaming. Perhaps every character she had met on the Camino was going to pass by this shop doorway and she would relive each brief encounter in a time warp.

'You do have somewhere to stay?' they sounded paternal.

'Yes. Thanks,' she offered the explanation, 'I was just resting.'

'Oh, that's ok then.' As they were leaving she saw a familiar pair of trousers approach from a different direction. She thought should stand and wake up properly.

Dominic pulled her to her feet and put his arms round her, 'What are you doing? Why did you go?'

'I was just tired.'

'Come on.' He was surprisingly tender. There was a small garden nearby that she had not seen and they went to sit on a bench and he kissed her.

'You like making love in public places,' she said softly.

'No,' he was annoyed, 'Who is here? And anyway why would they notice us? We are both adults.'

This was new territory; a sure way to shed the skin of the person she had become, ruled by conscience, the church, her upbringing. *That was in another country and besides the wench is dead.* She thought of honour and integrity; she thought of Seb as this other man whispered in her ear.

'You have walked the Camino; that is so special. You are strong you know. Now you can do anything.'

She sighed. Not ungrateful, but disbelieving.

'I will write to you from Holland. Perhaps I'll come and see you. We could meet up.'

'I'm not a free agent, Dominic. Nothing much has changed for women in the North of England at the fin de siècle. Nothing much has changed since the end of the last century. I will just go back home and everything will be just as it has been.'

'Things change when you make them change, or when you let them.'

'Dominic you are being very sweet. I had better go back to the hostel or they will lock me out.'

'I'll come with you.'

'No, I'll find my way now. I just got confused. You go back to your young people and your last night.'

She spoke without rancour or bitterness. She truly wanted him to go.

'Here is my email address. I have only given it to one or two special people. You have given yours to everyone who asked you. Will you really keep writing to all of them?'

She laughed. 'Maybe. And if you're really lucky.'

It was time to go.

THIRTY-FOUR

Rosemary overslept. Breakfast at the pilgrim's dining room was over by the time she woke. She was not surprised; she had been so tired and it had been late by the time she had finally fallen asleep. She turned her head first one way then the other to take out her earplugs. Most of the beds around her were still occupied, the occupants still not stirring even after she returned from the showers.

It felt good to have her rucksack on her back.

The path for Finisterra passed directly in front of the *Parador*. There was no sign of Murielle and Rafael. If they had stuck to their plan they would almost be in Finisterra by now. What a couple they made: a priest and a beauty. Each spoke their own language that neither understood. Harmony. Perhaps words are superfluous in the language of love.

She walked slowly all day; every step was an effort, every sinew protested, crying for rest. A distance of barely twenty kilometres felt like hundreds. She stopped frequently, although there were no villages along the way, collapsing by the path or on a fallen tree, sipping water from the heavy two-litre bottle till there was none left.

A flurry of text messages arrived with a jangle that interrupted birdsong. She stood still, desperate not to lose the signal. No sooner had she opened one than another pinged its arrival. First came old messages from Murielle. *Where are you?* Messages from the night before and one to say she and Rafael had overslept and hoped they would be forgiven. There was barely time to laugh before one came from Seb saying how much he missed her and how proud of her they were. She texted back to say thanks and that she had missed them too, but not everyday. She knew that honesty would be appreciated with a wry smile. When the phone rang she nearly dropped it. The useless gadget had played dead for almost the entire five hundred miles.

'Seb.'

She had no breath to talk. The blank sky settled quietly round, unrelieved by cloud or colour. His voice sounded so Northern after nearly a month. His sentences wove a net about her drawing her back home. Her heart fluttered in her chest like a trapped butterfly in a glass. She was pleased to hear him.

'A few more days,' she murmured.

Finally there was the day's destination. She came to the statue Dominic had described: of the fond family begging their father not to go to sea. To her it spoke of desertion and fear of destitution. The hostel lay two kilometres above the town, up hill all the way.

She lay down and slept as soon as she arrived. Surfacing later to think about what to eat as a young couple bustled about the kitchen as if they owned it.

'We can all eat together,' they said. Rosemary was grateful. She had meagre provisions of her own that could be added to the meal. She offered to help and the couple gave her a small task.

'We are walking because we love each other,' the girl said.

Rosemary was taken aback.

'The Camino is so beautiful; especially if you are in love. Don't you love the Camino?'

Rosemary's tongue stuck to the roof of her mouth and she could not form the words.

The young girl loved the Camino, her lover, the showers, the number seven, which happened to be the number staying in the hostel that night, slim ankles and her mother. Not necessarily in that order. Rosemary stayed to sit in the kitchen after the girl had trotted off. 'We are walking for love,' cropped up all round the hostel as if the girl was repeating a prayer and, whether anyone asked or not, she kept up her refrain, 'we are walking for love.'

The young man stayed at the large kitchen table and stared through the French window into the green field beyond. Rosemary wondered if the couple would even be friends when they reached Finisterra. If the young man did not feel inclined, and from the wistful look on his face it was conceivable he did, she personally would tape the girl's mouth.

After the meal, pasta and a dreary sauce, for which Rosemary was grateful, she went to bed. She did not think of love once and slept as if drugged.

The young couple waved goodbye to the small posse that left the hostel the following morning. They said they were not sure of their plans. There was a rush of sympathy for them and understanding in the sighs and 'ah well's'. The young couple who had been so annoying the night before and the butt of whispered jokes at their expense were, after all, to be pitied. They were not impervious to life's little unkindnesses; the sting in the tail of the beast called love. The consolation of the fall from grace was the softening of the hearts of their fellows. Out of love, the couple were more loveable.

The last day, by midday, pilgrims took off their shoes and walked along the coast over the expanse of white sand. They stopped to swim and could almost have paddled the rest of the way. The temptation to look for scallop shells (although there were none) and play in the warm, turquoise sea for hours made it late by

221

the time Rosemary arrived at the hostel in Finisterra. It was a rush then to buy bread and cheese for the picnic and walk to the coast, the furthest point west.

Light faded and she had to run because it was further than she thought and she was afraid she would miss the sunset. Once the sun began to fall its descent was rapid. Everyone else had got there before her. Spread around on the grass near the lighthouse at the end of the world, watching and waiting till the sky was magenta. Then it was pitch black and it was impossible to see anyone's face, only hear their voices softly murmuring. When the stars were high and the moon rose it was possible to see again and she straggled back with the others the way they had come.

There was a buzz at the hostel. Messages spreading like fire.

'Did you hear about the pilgrim?'

'I had a text message.'

'It was quite something, apparently.'

'The American girl was hysterical.'

Others gathered round in the dark of the kitchen where someone had thought to make cups of tea.

'Will someone just say what's happened?'

'You know the pilgrim they call the Flying Dutchman?'

Rosemary smiled, thinking how he would love being a living legend.

'Yes, I know him.'

'Of course she knows him, don't you remember?' The hint of a nudge.

'He had a heart attack and died on the way to the hospital. His body has to be flown home. The American girl who was with him had to be sedated and her parents are coming to get her.'

222

Already their voices were receding. Mouths moved, but she had ceased to hear what was said.

She pushed her way out of the hostel heading for the long curve of silver beach. The sea was way out. The moon reflected on the water in a shimmer. She followed the tide line where dots of seaweed loomed like dark pebbles in a fairy story to where the sea had deposited a scallop shell. In all the hours she had searched there had been nothing and here was the perfect shell, the emblem of pilgrims walking to Santiago. She picked it up, how comfortably it fitted her hand, turning it over and over, smoothing her fingers over its winged shoulders and ridged cape. The shell, the size of a human heart, warmed in her hand.

She thought of the table laid for Dominic's return with the empty place beside his mother, between the eleven brothers and sisters; the whole family gathered in grief, trying to fill the void by celebrating the life he'd had.

She lay on her back, consoled by the gentle lapping of the sea and saw the last star disappear before dawn. A new day. In the pocket of her shorts she felt the hard outline of Stefan's light meter; that fitted neatly in her hand too. She held it to her eye and tried to see the world anew.